KT-548-010

THE COLTONS

Welcome to Black Arrow, the birthplace of a proud, passionate branch of the Colton family, of men and women who would risk everything for love, family and honour.

Willow Colton: She hasn't told a soul about her 'predicament,' but soon she won't be able to hide her secret from her family…or the man responsible for her condition!

Tyler Chadwick: After an accident he's left with amnesia and a shadowy memory of a woman who touched his heart as no other lady had. He *must* find her…

Gloria WhiteBear: Will the secret past of this Coltons' matriarch come back to haunt her grandchildren?

Jesse Colton: His latest assignment could unlock the mystery of his family's past and be the key to finding true love.

Available in October 2003 from Silhouette Special Edition

Mercury Rising
by Christine Rimmer
(The Sons of Caitlin Bravo)

His Marriage Bonus
by Cathy Gillen Thacker
(The Deveraux Legacy)

The Cupcake Queen
by Patricia Coughlin

Willow in Bloom
by Victoria Pade
(The Coltons)

My Very Own Millionaire
by Pat Warren
(2-in-1)

The Woman for Dusty Conrad
by Tori Carrington

Willow in Bloom
VICTORIA PADE

SILHOUETTE®
SPECIAL EDITION™

DID YOU PURCHASE THIS BOOK WITHOUT A COVER?
If you did, you should be aware it is **stolen property** as it was
reported *unsold and destroyed* by a retailer. Neither the author nor
the publisher has received any payment for this book.

*All the characters in this book have no existence outside the imagination
of the author, and have no relation whatsoever to anyone bearing the
same name or names. They are not even distantly inspired by any
individual known or unknown to the author, and all the incidents are
pure invention.*

*All Rights Reserved including the right of reproduction in whole or in part
in any form. This edition is published by arrangement with Harlequin
Enterprises II B.V. The text of this publication or any part thereof may not
be reproduced or transmitted in any form or by any means, electronic or
mechanical, including photocopying, recording, storage in an
information retrieval system, or otherwise, without the written
permission of the publisher.*

*This book is sold subject to the condition that it shall not, by way of trade
or otherwise, be lent, resold, hired out or otherwise circulated without the
prior consent of the publisher in any form of binding or cover other than
that in which it is published and without a similar condition including
this condition being imposed on the subsequent purchaser.*

*Silhouette, Silhouette Special Edition and Colophon are
registered trademarks of Harlequin Books S.A., used under licence.*

*First published in Great Britain 2003
Silhouette Books, Eton House, 18-24 Paradise Road,
Richmond, Surrey TW9 1SR*

© Harlequin Books S.A. 2002

*Special thanks and acknowledgement are given to
Victoria Pade for her contribution to The Coltons series.*

ISBN 0 373 24490 8

23-1003

*Printed and bound in Spain
by Litografia Rosés S.A., Barcelona*

VICTORIA PADE

is a bestselling author of both historical and con-
temporary romance fiction, and the mother of two
energetic daughters, Cori and Erin. Although she
enjoys her chosen career as a novelist, she occasionally
laments that she has never travelled farther from her
Colorado home than Disneyland, instead spending all
her spare time plugging away at her computer. She
takes breaks from writing by indulging in her favourite
hobby—eating chocolate.

THE COLTONS: BLACK ARROW

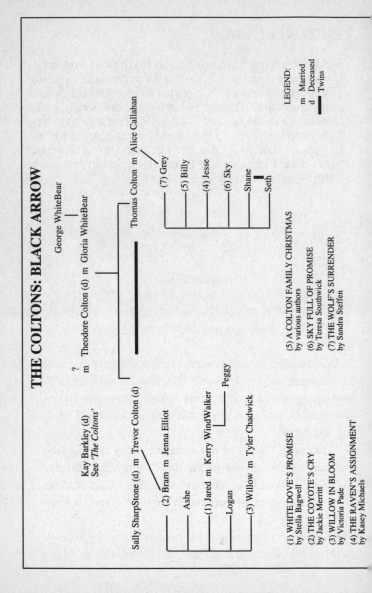

George WhiteBear

? m Theodore Colton (d) m Gloria WhiteBear

Kay Barkley (d)
See 'The Coltons'

Sally SharpStone (d) m Trevor Colton (d)

Thomas Colton m Alice Callahan

(2) Bram m Jenna Elliot
Ashe

(1) Jared m Kerry WindWalker
Peggy
Logan

(3) Willow m Tyler Chadwick

(7) Grey
(5) Billy
(4) Jesse
(6) Sky
Shane
Seth

(1) WHITE DOVE'S PROMISE
by Stella Bagwell

(2) THE COYOTE'S CRY
by Jackie Merritt

(3) WILLOW IN BLOOM
by Victoria Pade

(4) THE RAVEN'S ASSIGNMENT
by Kasey Michaels

(5) A COLTON FAMILY CHRISTMAS
by various authors

(6) SKY FULL OF PROMISE
by Teresa Southwick

(7) THE WOLF'S SURRENDER
by Sandra Steffen

LEGEND:
m Married
d Deceased
— Twins

Chapter One

"Willow, there's a guy... Willow? Are you *sleepin'*?"

Willow Colton woke with a start, dropping the bottle of vitamins in her hand. It rolled across her desk and she grabbed it in a hurry, hiding it in her lap as she tried to appear as if she hadn't just dozed off reading the label.

"Sleeping? No, I'm not sleeping. Why would I be sleeping in the middle of the day?" she said guiltily.

"Sure looked like you were sleepin'," Carl said, as if he still thought so but couldn't quite believe it himself.

Of course, there was good reason not to believe it. Willow ran Black Arrow Feed and Grain, the store her great-grandfather had founded, and she ordinarily put in longer and harder hours than anyone. Without napping in her office at the rear of the store.

But things were different these days.

"What were you saying when you came in?" she asked, changing the subject before it got to be a bigger deal than she wanted it to be. "That there's a guy..."

Carl's expression let her know he was suspicious, but he had no choice other than to concede. "There's a guy out here who wants to open a new account. Says he's the one bought the old Harris place."

"Ah," Willow said as she struggled to fight off the logy feeling of the impromptu snooze, hoping her desk blotter hadn't left an imprint on her face. "Ask him to wait just a few minutes and I'll be right with him. Please," she added, as if it would make this whole thing better.

"Sure," Carl replied, but his tone had a quizzical edge. And he sent her a curious glance over his shoulder as he left her office.

When he'd closed the door behind him, Willow deflated slightly, hoping she'd dodged the bullet and convinced her store manager that she hadn't been sleeping on the job.

She also tried to ignore the urge to put her head back on her desk so she could sleep again.

The fatigue was part of it, she knew now. The doctor she'd sneaked into Tulsa to see had assured her of that, so it didn't worry her anymore. But it *was* a nuisance. Especially when it interfered with work.

Work she needed to get back to.

With that in mind, she opened the left-hand drawer and slipped the vitamin bottle into it, closing it again with a resounding bang and making a mental note to take the vitamins upstairs to her apartment at the end of the day.

Then she stood and went to the tiny bathroom connected to the office to make sure she didn't look like she'd just gotten out of bed. That wouldn't do with a new customer. Or the old ones, for that matter.

The bathroom was barely that—a toilet and a sink crammed into a space the size of a closet. Willow had to avail herself of the facilities before she could even look in the mirror.

It was another of the current nuisances—her bladder seemed to have shrunk to the size of an acorn, and she spent every day hoping no one noticed how much more frequently she was having to go.

When she was finished, she stood at the sink and washed her hands, finally checking herself in the mirror.

She was glad to see there wasn't any evidence that she had dozed off. No imprints of desk accessories and no puffiness around her gray eyes.

Thank heaven for small favors. And maybe she really had been able to convince Carl that she hadn't been napping.

She was also glad to see that the now-usual morning pallor of her skin was gone, too. The Native American half of her bloodline had contributed a healthy looking reddish-brown complexion, but these days Willow started out nauseous and almost as pale as the O'Flannery sisters she'd gone to high school with. Not that there hadn't been a time during adolescence when she hadn't longed for the O'Flannerys' alabaster skin. But adulthood had brought with it an appreciation of her own heritage and all that went with it, including her color.

Plus she didn't want anything to give away her secret.

One well-arched eyebrow needed some smoothing, but not a strand of her long black hair had come free of the braid that fell to the middle of her back like a thick rope. Her lips were a natural pink that she'd only once added color to, and she had come to rue that occasion and the havoc it was wreaking on her life, so she'd thrown the lipstick away. But she did apply a little gloss just to keep her lips moist.

Her nap hadn't wrinkled her clothes—her blue jeans were fine and so was the plain blue, crew-neck T-shirt she wore tucked into them. As glad as she was that there were no signs of her nap, she was even more relieved that there was no evidence of the pregnancy, either. Her stomach was still as flat as ever. All in all, she judged herself presentable enough to meet her new customer.

If only she could stay awake through the meeting.

Hoping to aid that, she slapped her cheeks a little, the way they did in the movies to make people regain consciousness. It didn't help the feeling that she needed more sleep, but it did add color to her face, and that was a good thing. As good as it was going to get, she decided, leaving the bathroom to get back to business.

For a split second when she reentered her office, she forgot she'd put the telltale vitamins in her drawer, and felt a rush of panic at the thought that she might have left them out where someone could see them.

One glance at her desktop reminded her that she'd stashed them. So she crossed to the door that led to the sales room, opening it to greet the person she'd kept waiting.

Never in her wildest dreams would she have guessed who that person would be.

In fact, at first she thought she was seeing things.

She blinked, shook her head slightly and took a second look.

But she wasn't seeing things.

It was him.

It was him!

Her head began to spin.

Her breath caught in her throat.

Her knees buckled right out from under her.

"Whoa! Hold on there."

He reached out to catch her, but Willow landed with a shoulder against the doorjamb and managed to keep from falling without his help. Barely.

"I...I must have tripped," she muttered, in the weakest voice she'd ever heard come out of her mouth.

"You sure there isn't somethin' wrong with you today, Willow?" Carl asked from where he stood beside the man who had caused her shock. "Are you sick?"

"I'm fine," she insisted. "Just fine."

She eased herself away from the jamb, willing her knees to hold her as she did.

"You sure?" Carl persisted.

"I'm sure," she lied, knowing all the while that she was anything *but* fine.

"If you say so," her store manager muttered. Again disbelief rang in his tone, but he let it drop and said, "This here's Tyler Chadwick. Like I told you, he just bought the Harris place."

"I know who he is," Willow answered, wishing for more strength to her still breathy voice as she looked up into the face that had haunted her for the last two months. The face she hadn't been sure she'd ever see again. The face she hadn't been sure she *wanted* to see again.

"And this here's Willow Colton," Carl said to conclude the introductions. "She runs things 'round here, and it's her needs to tell you if you can open an account or not."

Willow… He knows me as Wyla….

But Tyler Chadwick didn't so much as blink an eye at the discrepancy. In fact, he smiled a perfectly open smile and said, "Pleased to meet you."

As if he'd never met her before.

Was he kidding? He'd been quite a tease, as she recalled, so maybe he was just putting her on.

But something about the way he was looking at her, at the blankness in his expression, said he wasn't kidding at all. That he didn't remember her.

"Wyla…" she said under her breath, to jolt his memory.

"Wyla?" he repeated. "Or Willow? Did I hear wrong?"

"Wyla?" Carl echoed, overhearing Tyler's response. "Her name's Willow." Then to Willow he said, "What's goin' on with you today?"

Willow didn't answer that because she couldn't. She just stood there, staring at Tyler Chadwick.

And it *was* Tyler Chadwick. For a moment she had entertained the idea that maybe this man was just someone who looked remarkably like him. And happened to have the same name.

But of course, that was crazy. This was definitely the Tyler Chadwick she knew. Granted, she'd spent just a short time with him, but it had been a memorable time. He was a memorable man.

He wasn't terribly tall—only about five feet ten, a scant three inches taller than she was. But it was an impressive five ten of hard muscles honed from making his living riding bucking broncos on the rodeo circuit.

There wasn't an ounce of fat on that body, made up of broad shoulders, narrow waist and hips, and biceps and thighs that bulged beneath his tan-colored shirt and jeans respectively.

And even if any of that had changed in the last two months, his face hadn't. It was still handsome enough to make the birds stop singing in the trees just to get a look at him when he walked by.

He had light-brown hair cut short on the sides and left sort of haphazardly spiky on top; a sharp chiseled jaw; a supple mouth Adonis would have envied; a thin, straight nose; deep-set eyes that were so vibrant a green they looked more like emeralds beneath slightly bushy brows and a full, square forehead.

And when he smiled—even just a little—he had one dimple, one deep crease in the middle of his left cheek, that made him look mischievous and dashing and deliciously dangerous all at once.

Oh no, she wasn't mistaken. This was Tyler Chadwick. The one and only Tyler Chadwick. The unmistakable Tyler Chadwick.

He wasn't someone she could forget.

Which, unfortunately, didn't seem to be something he could say about her.

Unless maybe he thought she might be embarrassed if anyone found out she already knew him and how, and he was trying to spare her that by pretending they were just meeting for the first time…?

That must be it, she concluded.

"Why don't you come into the office," Willow suggested, thinking that once they were alone he would let her know he was merely being considerate of her feelings by making it seem as if he didn't already have intimate knowledge of her.

Tyler shot a glance at Carl and said, "Thanks for your help." Then he turned those oh-so-striking green eyes back on Willow.

She got lost in them for a moment before she realized he wasn't looking meaningfully into her face, he was merely waiting for her to move out of the doorway so they could go into her office.

"This way," she said unnecessarily, mentally yanking herself into line as she turned to go back the way she'd come.

She heard the click of his boot heels behind her, but he didn't close the door to allow them privacy.

"Oh, we should have shut the door," she said, as if it had just occurred to her.

"Okay."

He backtracked to do that, then joined her at her desk.

Willow pointed to one of the visitors chairs and took her own seat on the opposite side of the gray metal desk before she said, "Okay, the coast is clear."

Tyler smiled that dimpled smile, but his brows pulled together in a show of confusion. "The coast is clear for what? Talkin' money?"

If he was playing dumb, this was taking it too far.

Or did he really not remember her?

She searched his glorious green eyes for any sign of recognition.

But it honestly wasn't there. Not a hint of it. Not

one iota. Not so much as an indication that he thought she looked vaguely familiar, and was trying to figure out where he'd seen her before.

How was that possible?

He hadn't been drinking that night. Even though they'd met in a blues club where liquor was flowing like water, he'd been ordering ginger ale. So she knew alcohol wasn't to blame.

But then it occurred to her that not only did Tyler know her as Wyla—the nickname her old friend Becky Lindstrom had called her all through college and used that night—but Willow had also looked considerably different.

Thanks to Becky's makeover, her hair had been loose and her face had been made up—complete with lipstick. And she'd been wearing one of Becky's dresses—a form-fitting little red number Willow would never have had the courage to buy, let alone wear at any other time.

She definitely hadn't looked the way she did today. Or any other day or night before or after that fateful evening she'd met Tyler Chadwick.

So maybe that was the problem. Maybe without the face paint, with her hair tied back, dressed in jeans and a T-shirt, introduced to him by another name, and in an entirely different setting, she looked so different that he just wasn't putting two and two together.

And maybe if she helped with that two and two he might see past the surface and add it all up.

With that in mind, she said, "So are you on hiatus from rodeo riding?"

"That's right, you said you know who I am, didn't you? You follow the circuit?" he asked.

"No, but I saw you ride in Tulsa in June. Mid-June. On a Friday night..." Of course, when she and Becky had met him in that bar much later that evening they'd pretended they *hadn't* seen the rodeo and didn't know who he was. Just to give him a hard time.

So that wasn't much of a hint.

"There was a packed crowd that night," he was saying as Willow worked to pay attention. "Standing room only. You must have had your tickets a long while in advance. Was that your first time?"

"Yes." For the rodeo. And only the second for what came later that night....

"It was my next-to-last," he said quietly, soberly.

Willow sensed that she'd hit on a sore subject. "Did you retire?" she asked, using the term facetiously, since he was hardly retirement age.

But all he said in answer was, "Something like that."

It was clear he didn't want to talk about it, and because it wasn't getting her any nearer her goal, anyway, she didn't pursue it. Instead she decided to try a different tack.

"I suppose you must have met a lot of people along the way."

"Probably more than my fair share."

"A lot of women."

He smiled wryly. "Probably more than my fair share."

Willow acknowledged that with a raise of her chin, but began to give in to the inevitable thought she'd been trying to avoid—that she had been just one of many. That that night, so unlike anything she had ever done in her life, had been so commonplace to him that he didn't even remember it.

"So you got around pretty good, did you?" she heard herself say before she even knew she was going to. In a very accusatory tone.

"I didn't have a different woman every night of the week, if that's what you're asking, no. But what does that have to do with opening an account for feed?"

Good question.

Willow had to think fast to come up with an answer.

"I was just wondering if you'd settled down with a wife or a girlfriend who would also be on the account."

Feeble. Oh, was that feeble.

But it was the best she could do on the spot.

And he didn't really buy it. She could see the doubt in his expression.

But he went along with it, anyway.

"No, there's just me. I'll be the only one on the account. Shouldn't you be writing something down?"

Willow felt even more stupid—if that were possible—because he was right, she hadn't so much as taken out a piece of paper or a pencil.

She did that now, filling in his name at the top of the form she used.

"You'll have to give me the formal address. I know the Harris place, but I don't know the numbers off the top of my head," she said, trying hard to sound businesslike to counteract her total unprofessionalism up to that point.

Tyler rattled off the route number and zip code, and as Willow wrote those down, too, she worked to come up with more questions or conversation that might spur his memory without seeming completely inappropriate.

But she couldn't think of anything, and instead just asked the usual things about his finances, references, and about how much feed and grain he thought he'd be needing per month.

And then the form was finished and all that was left was for him to sign it to authorize her to run a credit check on him.

When he'd done that, he stood. "Guess that takes care of it then."

A sudden feeling of panic rushed through Willow at the thought that he was on the verge of leaving and she hadn't made any headway whatsoever in getting him to remember her.

"So did you end up taking home all the prize money that weekend in Tulsa?" she asked in a last-ditch effort, hoping any mention of Tulsa or that weekend might spur something in him.

But it just seemed to dampen his mood again. "No,

only Friday's purse. The competition you must have seen,'' he said, once more sounding as if he didn't want to talk about it.

And maybe that was the problem, Willow thought. Maybe losing the following two days had caused him to block out the entire weekend. Her included.

Not that that made it any more heartening as she finally gave in and admitted she was failing miserably at making him remember her.

''You'll let me know once you get the credit report and okay the account, so I can put in an order?'' he asked as he made his way to the office door with Willow following him this time.

''I'll be in touch,'' she assured him, unable to keep her own dismay out of her voice.

Apparently he heard it, because he tossed her a small frown. But he didn't question it. He just said, ''I'll be lookin' forward to hearing from you. And to doing business with you.''

Willow could only manage a nod, at which point he headed down the main aisle and left the store.

And as she stood in her office doorway again and watched him go, she couldn't quite believe what had just happened.

The one man she'd done something totally outrageous and uncharacteristic with, the one time in her life she'd ever done anything totally outrageous and uncharacteristic at all, had just strolled in, apparently without a single memory of ever even having met her.

And she didn't know what to do about it.

It was so humiliating.

So humiliating that she wished that night they'd spent together could be left a secret she could carry with her to her grave, so no one would ever be the wiser. So her humiliation would never be known.

She wished she could steer clear of Tyler Chadwick for the rest of her life, in spite of those eyes and that face and that body.

And as she retreated back into her office and closed the door once again, she considered doing just that— steering clear of Tyler Chadwick for the rest of her life.

But she wasn't sure that was the right thing to do. Even if he was the kind of creep who spent the night with a woman and then forgot all about it. All about her.

Because even if he was that kind of creep, even if he didn't remember having met her, it didn't change the fact that he had. That he'd done much, much more than just meet her.

It didn't change the fact that she was now pregnant with his baby.

Chapter Two

"I'm sitting on my front porch with my feet up on the railing, drinking a steaming cup of coffee and watchin' the sun rise. How's that compare to a smelly motel room, a stale Danish and a cup of weak, luke-warm swill that's supposed to pass for a cup a' joe?"

"Mornin', big brother," the voice on the other end of the phone said when Tyler had finished his lengthy greeting. "Tryin' to make me jealous, are you?"

"Yup."

"Well, it's workin'. This room smells like mildew, my complimentary continental breakfast is a muffin you could play hardball with, and I think the coffee was made yesterday."

"And I wish I was there," Tyler added, slightly under his breath.

Brick didn't comment on that, and Tyler knew his younger brother didn't know what to say to it.

But Brick didn't let much silence lapse before he used Tyler's utterance as a segue. "How're you feeling?"

"Okay. The headaches are still comin' but they're fewer and farther between, and the pills help when they do hit."

"That's something. What about the other? Are things clearin' up on that front?"

"No. That's the same."

"And you haven't found your mystery woman to help?"

His mystery woman. The woman he'd met at a blues club and spent that last night with. Whoever she was...

"If I have found my mystery woman it hasn't helped," Tyler said with a laugh to lighten the tone. "No, seriously, I've only met one woman—someone named Willow Colton. She runs the feed and grain store here and she isn't my mystery woman."

"Because she didn't spark anything? You know what the doctors said about your theory that—"

"Not only because she didn't spark anything. She recognized me from Tulsa in June because she was at the rodeo Friday afternoon and saw me ride."

"So she's not the one."

"*And* she didn't spark anything, so, no, she's not the one," Tyler said definitively.

But talking about Willow Colton brought her to Tyler's mind. Vividly to mind. Something that had been happening every time he turned around since meeting her the day before.

She might not be his mystery woman, but she'd certainly struck a note with him. Of course, that shouldn't have come as any surprise. After all, she was beautiful, so she would have struck a note with anyone. Beautiful with shiny licorice-black hair and skin as smooth as satin. High, broad cheekbones; a sweet little nose. Full, luscious lips the color of Colorado's red rocks. And those eyes—luminous, ethereal, pale, pale dove-gray—those eyes could mesmerize a man....

"You're probably right." Brick's voice broke into Tyler's wandering thoughts. "Not only isn't Miss Feed and Grain your mystery woman if she was at the rodeo, but if she'd been with you that night she'd have said it."

"That's what I'm figuring, too. Besides, I don't care what the doctors or anyone else say, I think I'll know her when I see her. I just feel it in my gut."

Brick didn't comment on that, either. He didn't have to. They'd had this conversation a dozen times in the last two months, and Tyler knew his brother thought he had just gone a little crazy in response to an unwanted life change. He also knew that in many ways Brick was merely humoring him, figuring he'd come to his senses eventually.

But Brick did look on the bright side. "Well, one way or another, that pull you felt to Black Arrow landed you a nice piece of property. If nothin' else, maybe fate was planting *that* seed to get you where you were meant to go.''

"So when are you comin' to stay awhile?''

"You miss me. Admit it, you really miss me,'' Brick goaded.

"Yeah, I miss all that snoring and snortin' you do in your sleep every night,'' Tyler countered facetiously, when in truth he did miss his brother. Not only had they shared a bedroom their entire growing up years, but since they'd left home to follow the rodeo circuit they'd rarely been apart.

But Tyler knew there was no way he'd ever live it down if he admitted that he actually did miss Brick.

"I'll be there the weekend after next,'' his brother said in answer to his question. "And don't go thinkin' I'll be able to recognize the mystery woman if we come across her, either, because I keep tellin' you that I didn't so much as cast her a glance before I left you with her in that bar. I was too tired to think straight that night.''

"Yeah, yeah, I've heard it before.''

"I just wish to hell I'd made you come back to the room with me instead of leaving you there. Then maybe you wouldn't have still been thinkin' about her the next day and you wouldn't have been distracted and—''

"We all get dealt our own hand, little brother, and that was mine,'' Tyler said in answer to the suddenly serious tone Brick had taken.

"Yeah, well, still and all—''

"Still and all nothin'. Things happen the way they're supposed to happen." Whether it's easy to understand or cope with or not.

Tyler heard the sound of a knock on his brother's motel room door just before Brick said, "That's the guys."

"Headin' out for a real breakfast," Tyler added, knowing the routine well himself. And suffering a terrible pang not to be a part of it anymore.

But he didn't let it sound in his voice. He made sure to seem upbeat. "You better get goin' or they'll leave you behind. I just wanted to wish you luck on your ride tonight. Let me know how you do."

Brick wasn't as good at hiding his feelings. His voice echoed with sadness. "You know I will. Talk to you later."

"Talk to you later," Tyler answered. Then he pushed the button to disconnect the call, and set his cordless phone on the planked floor of his front porch.

"Damn," he muttered to himself, weathering the fresh surge of sorrow that flooded through him.

But things were the way they were, he reminded himself. They couldn't be changed, and pining for what used to be, for what might have been if only, didn't help anything. He needed to look to the positives, not the negatives.

Like the fact that he was now the owner of this ranch and had a home of his own.

Like the fact that even if it was sooner than he'd planned, this was still the life he and Brick had always talked about having when they were ready to throw in the towel on bronc busting.

Like the fact that Black Arrow was a nice, quiet town full of friendly people.

People like Willow Colton.

Willow Colton whose legs went on for miles, whose tight body couldn't have been better proportioned, and whose breasts were just the right size to fit into a man's hands....

Tyler knew what his brother would say about Willow Colton if he saw her. Brick would say, "Who needs a mystery woman when there's a flesh and blood woman like Willow Colton?"

But Brick didn't understand what was going on inside Tyler over his mystery woman.

Hell, Tyler didn't understand it himself.

He just knew there was something pushing him to find her. And maybe to find that part of himself that he'd lost in the process.

And he didn't think he could rest until he did.

Even if he was having trouble getting that image of Miss Feed and Grain out of his head.

Even if he was looking forward to seeing her again more than he wanted to.

No, his mystery woman was like lost pages in a book he just had to finish, and until he figured out who she was, he was damn sure not starting up anything with anyone else.

Not even a woman with pale dove-gray eyes that seemed to haunt him.

Because no matter how much that might be the case, those pale-gray eyes didn't haunt him as much as that gap his mystery woman had left.

And he was all about filling that gap.

Willow hadn't slept much the night before, which didn't help her fatigue. But even feeling more tired than usual, she was at no risk of falling asleep at her desk the way she had on Tuesday. The same thoughts that had kept her awake until the wee hours of the morning kept her adrenaline level high through Wednesday.

Tyler Chadwick was on her mind. Tyler Chadwick and the predicament she was in.

Not that Tyler and her predicament had been far from her thoughts at any point in the two months before this. But since he'd walked into her life again nearly twenty-four hours ago, she had been completely incapable of thinking about anything else.

She also hadn't been able to stop asking herself the same two questions—how could he have forgotten her, and how could he have forgotten their night together?

It was just so awful to think that he had.

She wasn't proud of what she'd done in Tulsa. In fact, she'd been ashamed of herself. Spending the night with someone she'd just met in a club? That was definitely a first. And a last.

But it was as if something had snapped in her in June.

It hadn't been easy growing up with four older

brothers. Four very protective older brothers. But since Willow had been out on her own, running the Feed and Grain, one or another of her brothers was at her side every time she turned around. Watching over her to the point where she felt as if she were being stalked by her own family.

She'd tried talking to them, reasoning with them, letting them know she wasn't doing anything even remotely dangerous and that they did not need to take turns becoming her ever-present guardians.

But no sooner had she given that lecture than there they were again. Just checking in with her, they said.

Until, finally, Willow had thought she might explode.

She'd known if she didn't get away from them for a while she was going to lose her temper and say things that would hurt their feelings. And she didn't want that.

So Willow had called her friend Becky Lindstrom in Tulsa and taken her up on her repeated request for Willow to visit.

Just for a week. A week of rest and relaxation, with no brothers looking over her shoulder every minute. That's all it was supposed to be. That's all it was.

Until Friday.

Friday night when she knew her week was at an end and she had to go back to Black Arrow, back to four brothers who couldn't leave her alone.

Just the thought of that had left her feeling the need to go a little wild. To cut loose one last time before she went back. To get out and do something she wouldn't do at home. To be someone besides a person with four brothers who seemed to need to keep her in a velvet cage.

So, on their way home from an afternoon at the rodeo that was passing through Tulsa at the time, Willow had confided her feelings to Becky.

Becky had embraced the idea with a vengeance. A night on the town. Just the two of them. Kicking up their heels.

Becky had reveled in the free hand to make Willow over. To doll her up in a way Willow never got dolled up. To transform her into a new woman.

No jeans.

No T-shirts or flannels.

No practical shoes.

No braided hair.

Becky had loaned Willow a slinky, strapless red dress that fit every inch of the few inches it covered like a second skin.

Spike-heeled shoes had gone with it, but Becky hadn't stopped at merely outfitting Willow. She'd also played beauty shop with Willow's hair, with makeup Willow never wore, with perfume and lipstick that were the finishing touches that turned everyday Willow Colton into exotic Wyla and made her feel truly like a different person.

Out on the town.

Nightclubbing.

And that's where Willow had met Tyler Chadwick. At a blues club.

She and Becky had recognized him from the rodeo earlier in the evening. He was one of the bronco riders. The drop-dead gorgeous bronco rider with the derriere to die for. The one who had won.

By that time, Becky had had enough champagne to lower all her inhibitions, and she'd suggested they invite him to join them.

Willow, who had been feeling no pain herself, hadn't put up too much of a fight.

"Just don't let him know we know who he is," Becky had whispered to Willow before leaving their table. "He'll get a swelled head if he thinks we think he's somebody."

And that's how it had happened.

Tyler Chadwick had taken them up on the offer and joined them.

But from the minute he sat down, his focus had been on Willow.

Or actually, on Wyla.

Becky hadn't minded. Not long after it had become clear that Tyler Chadwick preferred Willow, another man had begun to show an interest in Becky, and she'd gone to sit at the bar with him, leaving Willow and Tyler alone.

Wyla and Tyler.

Which was when Willow had discovered that her new Wyla persona could be quite a flirt.

And not only that, she could be coy and cute and coquettish, too.

She could even be sexy.

It had all seemed innocent enough. It had been Wyla doing it, not her. Wyla who was laughing that high-pitched laugh. Wyla who was putting her hand on Tyler's arm. Wyla who was drinking so much champagne…

It wasn't completely clear in Willow's mind how she'd gone from that innocent flirtation in the bar to Tyler Chadwick's room in the hotel next door. But that was where she'd ended up. In the suite he and his brother were sharing, because of some glitch in their reservation that had upgraded them.

Which meant that he had a bedroom to himself.

A bedroom in which he and Willow—Wyla—had had a wild night of passion.

Mindless passion, as Willow's head had been filled only with thoughts of Tyler Chadwick and all he was doing to her that made her feel so, so good.

So, so unlike herself.

So unlike herself that after a second round of lovemaking just after the sun had come up, when Tyler had fallen asleep again, she hadn't been able to believe what she'd done.

It wasn't merely uncharacteristic behavior. It was complete insanity.

And while Tyler still slept, Willow—and she had been Willow again by then—had dressed at record speed and slipped out of that hotel room, out of that hotel and into a cab, putting that night and Tyler Chadwick behind her.

Which was exactly where she intended to leave them. Forever.

Then she'd missed her period.

At first she'd thought it was just stress, but when she'd begun to have some very odd symptoms that couldn't have been stress-related she'd had to entertain the possibility that something else was going on.

Pregnancy.

She'd actually passed out cold in the doctor's office when her worst fear was confirmed.

And then she'd come to and cried. Sobbed. Right in front of the doctor.

That had caused the doctor to talk about alternatives if she didn't want the child, which had made Willow cry all the harder.

"Alternatives? I don't have any alternatives," she'd wailed.

But by the time she'd returned to Black Arrow that night she'd thought about the alternatives the doctor had laid out for her and she'd known she couldn't choose any of them. This was *her* baby and she was going to have it, raise it, love it.

She just didn't know anything else.

She didn't know how she was going to have and raise a child alone.

She didn't know how she was going to tell her brothers.

She didn't know what they were going to do when she did.

She didn't know whether or not she should find Tyler Chadwick and tell him.

Only now he'd found her.

He just didn't know it.

Willow slumped in her desk chair like a wilting flower.

The father of her baby was a man who obviously had had so many one-night stands with so many different women that he didn't even remember the women he'd had them with.

It kept coming back to that.

Back to what Willow had thought the previous day—that he was the worst kind of creep.

But he hadn't *seemed* like a creep that night in Tulsa.

She'd thought he was the nicest guy she'd ever met.

He'd made her laugh. He'd put her at ease. He'd made her feel good about herself. He'd made her feel free. Free from being the little sister to Bram and Ashe and Jared and Logan.

Which had been exactly what she'd needed.

It had just been so wonderful it had all apparently gone to her head.

"But that was then and this is now," she said to herself as she crossed her arms on her desk and laid her head on them to rest.

And as much as she wished she could just forget

about Tyler Chadwick and that night, the way he apparently had, she couldn't.

So what *was* she going to do? she asked herself.

One thing that she definitely couldn't see herself doing was marching up to him and announcing out of the blue that, whether he remembered it or not, they'd slept together and that she was pregnant as a result.

But what if she gave him more of a chance to remember her? What if she did what she could to spend some time with him? To let him get to know her? To see more of her?

Maybe something about the sound of her voice or the way she looked at just the right angle would make him remember her and that night together.

Surely somewhere in his brain there was some image of her that could be brought back to the surface.

And then…

And then…

She didn't know what then.

But at least it was a first step. It was something to do.

And she *needed* to do something. Something that could give her a clue as to where to go from here.

Because not only had Willow been knocked for a loop when she found out she was pregnant, she didn't have the faintest idea what to do about breaking the news to her brothers, or whether or not to tell the baby's father, or what to expect his reaction would be if she did, or what to do about her entire future.

But getting the baby's father to remember the baby's mother seemed like a logical beginning.

She just hoped that her initial impression of Tyler as a genuinely nice guy had had some validity to it and that he wasn't really the jerk she'd decided he was the day before. That maybe along the way he'd tell her she reminded him of someone he'd once encountered, and she would learn that he hadn't forgotten her at all, that he just hadn't connected the dots and realized that she and Wyla were the same person.

It was a hope she tried hard to hang on to even though she was very much afraid the odds were against her.

But still it was a whole lot better to hope that his not knowing her had a simple, believable explanation than to accept what seemed more likely—that he'd spent an entire night making love to her and now didn't remember who she was.

Willow had the perfect excuse to see Tyler again, and once she'd closed up the Feed and Grain for the day she decided to use it.

But not before making a stop in the apartment above the store.

The apartment had been her grandmother's, but Willow had moved into it with Gloria when Willow had taken over the running of the Feed and Grain. Now that her grandmother had passed away she lived there alone.

And she never climbed the stairs at the back of the

store without wishing she would still find her grandmother there to greet her.

But she was learning to weather those moments, and tonight, when she had, she made a beeline for her own bedroom to change her clothes.

Only as she stood in her closet, trying to figure out what to change into that might give Tyler a hint as to who she was, did it occur to her that all of her things were basically the same—jeans and tops.

She had a couple of pairs of slacks she wore to church, and a plain, simple black dress that she wore with a matching jacket to funerals and, without the jacket, to weddings. But that was about it. And because she knew she'd feel overdressed if she wore her Sunday slacks—besides the fact that it would no doubt raise eyebrows and questions if anyone who knew her saw her—the closest she could come to Wyla-wear was a red V-neck T-shirt with a clean pair of jeans.

She did unbraid her hair, though, brushing it and letting it fall free the way she'd worn it that night. And although lip gloss was all she owned in the way of makeup, she made a mental note to buy herself a few cosmetics as soon as possible to aid her cause.

Then she locked up the apartment and used the outside stairs to go down to her old blue pickup truck, wishing she had a better, sexier vehicle, too.

But there wasn't anything to be done about it, and so she climbed behind the wheel, started the engine and pulled away from the curb, feeling more anxious than she could ever remember having felt before.

Willow was familiar with all the farms and ranches around Black Arrow. It had been her job at the Feed and Grain to make deliveries after school as soon as she'd been old enough to drive. So she knew exactly where she was going.

The former Harris place was south of town about four miles. She'd gone all through school with the Harrises' only child, Samantha. But she and Willow hadn't been friends. Samantha had been a very girly girl—worlds apart from tomboy Willow.

As she turned off the main road onto the private drive she could see the house in the distance. It was a two-story frame, painted white and trimmed in black, with a steep black roof.

The house had a nice front porch—that was what Willow had always liked best about it. The porch was bordered with a spindled railing that looked beautiful at Christmas, decorated with lights and evergreen boughs.

But August was not the time for that, and other than a wicker rocker and a chair swing hanging from chains, the porch itself was littered with several moving boxes apparently waiting to be thrown out.

No lights shone through the windows, but since it was only seven o'clock and there was still an abundance of summer daylight, Willow didn't think that was a sign that no one was home. Besides, there was a big white truck parked in the drive, so she assumed Tyler was there.

She parked beside the truck and cut her engine, taking a deep breath to bolster her courage and wishing—as she had so many times since June—that things hadn't taken the turn they had.

But wishing didn't make any of it go away, so she picked up the file she'd brought with her as her excuse, and got out of the truck to climb the five steps onto the porch.

The front door was open, and through the screen door she could hear music playing. Softly.

She recognized the singer. Chris Isaak. He was one of her favorites, and she hoped that maybe he was one of Tyler's favorites, too, and the fact that they shared similar musical tastes was a good sign.

She knocked on the screen's frame, feeling her tension level increase with each rap.

Nothing stirred in response. Chris Isaak just went on singing about the wicked things people do.

Maybe she hadn't knocked loud enough to be heard over the music. She tried again with more force.

"Hold on," she heard Tyler call, his unmistakable baritone sounding as if it were coming from the living room to the right of the front door.

Then he came into sight from that direction.

He had on a white T-shirt, a pair of jeans with a tear in the knee, and he was in his stocking feet.

He was hardly dressed for company, yet he still looked good enough to make Willow recall one of the reasons she'd been so swept off her feet by him in Tulsa. The man exuded a raw sensuality that made the woman in her sit up and take notice.

She, on the other hand, didn't seem to have the same effect on him. The way he squinted his eyes against the light made it look as if he'd been sleeping.

"I'm sorry if I disturbed you," Willow said, as that thought occurred to her.

"No, no, it's okay," he assured her, blinking a few times as if fighting to keep his eyes open. "I just had one of these headaches I get, and the pills for them knock me out."

"Maybe I should come back another time."

He waved away that notion with one big, blunt-fingered hand. "Nah. It's fine. Headache's gone."

He pinched the bridge of his nose and then took his hand away and finally seemed to really look at her.

"Willow. Willow Colton. From the feed store," she stated.

"I know," he answered. But then he gave her the once-over and smiled that one-sided smile. "You look different than you did yesterday, but I still knew you."

From yesterday, but not from June...

She tried not to let that bother her.

Tyler stepped back from the doorway. "Come on in."

Willow hesitated a moment, feeling all the more awkward because she'd awakened him. But in the end she decided that, since she already had, she might as well do what she'd come for.

"If you're sure."

"Positive. I'm glad for the company. Gets kind of lonely out here."

Willow accepted his invitation and went in.

It was cooler inside than out, and the scent of leather was in the air. Maybe from the cowboy boots that stood beside the wide, elegant staircase that faced the door.

Tyler didn't seem to mind being shoeless in front of her because he didn't move to put the boots back on. Instead he just closed the door and pointed toward the living room.

"Let's go in there."

Willow did, with Tyler following behind.

"Excuse the mess," he said in reference to the fact that lamps were on the floor rather than on tables, and chairs were in no particular arrangement. The only pieces of furniture that were situated with any sort of purpose were the long leather sofa—likely the source of the scent of the place—and a wide-screen television.

"Please, sit down," he invited. "Can I get you something to drink? Iced tea?"

"No, thank you," Willow responded. Her throat felt like the top of a drawstring bag with the ties cinched so tight she didn't think she could get even liquids down.

She did sit on the couch, though. Hugging one end.

"I just wanted to let you know you'd been approved for an account with us and to bring you over our price lists and policies," she announced, not sounding nearly as relaxed as he seemed to feel.

"Great. I appreciate that," he said, joining her on

the sofa at the opposite end, as if he were entertaining an insurance salesman.

Willow opened the file folder she was clutching in a white-knuckled grip, and pointed out a few details about special orders and delivery schedules. It didn't take long, and once she'd finished, she realized she'd exhausted her excuse to be there.

"Maybe I will have that glass of iced tea, after all," she said, to give herself more of a reason to linger and put into motion her plan to spend time with him.

"Sounds good to me, too," he said.

"If you're sure you're up to it," she added.

"I'm fine."

All remnants of his nap had disappeared, and he seemed as awake and energized as ever, so she believed him.

"Can I help?" she asked as he stood.

"You can keep me company, but I think I can manage the pouring myself," he joked.

Willow got to her feet, too, tagging along.

As she did, her gaze took a dip to his derriere, and she realized her own memory hadn't done it justice.

But that was the last thing she needed to be thinking about, so she forced her eyes to behave, and made small talk to occupy her mind.

"When I was a teenager my job was to make our deliveries. Mr. Harris would have me come in as far as the living room while he signed the receipt. I've never seen the rest of the house, though."

"I'll give you the grand tour," Tyler promised.

''But be warned, there isn't much to see. Before this I lived in a studio apartment, and I was only there when I wasn't chasing rodeos. So I didn't have a lot to bring with me to fill this place up.''

They went through a large, empty dining room before they passed under an archway to get to the kitchen. The very white kitchen. Walls, cupboards and appliances were all sterile, hospital white, and there wasn't a single other color to break the almost blinding, institutional effect.

Apparently that fact wasn't lost on Tyler. As he went to the refrigerator he said, ''You just about need sunglasses in here.''

''Just about,'' Willow agreed.

Tyler poured two glasses of iced tea and asked if Willow wanted sugar in hers. When she declined, he handed her one of the glasses and then they set out for the tour of the house.

He was right about there being nothing much to see. There were four bedrooms, three baths and a recreation room upstairs; another bathroom, a den and a library to go with the kitchen, living room and dining room downstairs. But room after room was bare, except for beds in two of the bedrooms, and a few unpacked boxes here and there.

''You weren't kidding when you said you didn't bring much with you,'' she said as they returned to the living room. Tyler had pointed in the direction of the sofa with his chin, inviting Willow to sit down again.

"I know," he said with a laugh that transported her back to that night in Tulsa, when they'd both done a lot of laughing and the sound of his deep, full-barreled chuckle had sent a skitter of delight along her spine. Just as it did now.

Then he added, "And I don't have any idea where to start to furnish the place. Or where to even look for things in Black Arrow."

"We actually have a furniture store. With some factory-manufactured things and some really nice hand-crafted pieces that folks around town make," she informed him.

She knew this was a prime opening, but it took a moment of screwing up her courage to take advantage of it. "I'd be happy to go with you, show you where it is, give you my opinion—for what it's worth."

"I might just take you up on that. I could definitely use a woman's advice when it comes to decorating."

Not many men in Black Arrow thought of her as a woman. It pleased Willow to no end that Tyler did.

But she tried to contain her pleasure. She didn't want to appear too eager.

"So where are you from?" she asked, changing the subject before she got carried away. And also because when she'd found out she was pregnant she'd realized she'd actually learned next to nothing about him that night in Tulsa, and thought it was time she did.

"I was born and raised in Wyoming," he answered.

"Is that where your family is?"

"My folks died in a flood up there a few years back.

That left only me and my brother, Brick. Brick is still riding the rodeo circuit, and since I bought this place we gave up the apartment we shared in Cheyenne. When he needs a place to stay off the road he'll come here.''

''Your brother wasn't ready to retire with you?'' Willow asked.

''No. Neither was I, for that matter,'' he added with that same regret he'd had in his voice the day before, when they'd talked about this.

''Then why did you?'' Willow persisted, hoping he didn't think she was prying. Even though she was.

Tyler didn't answer right away. He took a drink of his iced tea and stared into the glass.

And the longer he hesitated, the more she began to worry that he *did* think she was prying, and didn't like it.

But then he set his glass on the floor beside the sofa and raised his amazing green eyes to her. ''You said you were at Friday's rodeo in Tulsa. Well, that was my last good ride. On Saturday I got thrown. I landed on my head and ended up with a concussion that put me in a coma for fifteen days. Nobody was too sure I was going to come out of it or, if I did, whether I'd be okay. When I finally did regain consciousness the doctors said no more bronc bustin'. So that was it for me.''

''I'm sorry,'' Willow said, because she could see what a blow that news had been to him. But for herself, she felt a strange sense of relief. She'd seen how dangerous what he did was, and the thought of her baby's father doing it had apparently bothered her more than she'd realized.

"Luckily, I'd been socking away prize and endorsement money for a lot of years," Tyler continued. "So I bought this place and came here to settle down."

"How did you end up choosing Black Arrow for that?" she asked, since when she'd told him that fateful June night that this was where she lived, he'd never heard of it before.

Tyler laughed again and inclined his head in a way that made Willow think he was confused by the choice himself.

Then he confirmed that by saying, "I don't know for sure how I chose Black Arrow. Here's the thing, the concussion blanked out some of my memory. It left me with some holes. When it came time to pick a place to settle down, Black Arrow popped into my head. I'm pretty sure it's connected to some other things I've forgotten, things I'm trying to remember, but one way or another, something about it just seemed right. Right enough so that I contacted a Realtor here and bought this place sight unseen."

"You lost your memory?" Willow asked, seizing on that part of what he'd said because it was so vital to her.

"Not all of it. Mostly I'm blank about things that happened in the weeks just before the accident."

"People, too?"

"Places I'd been, rodeos I'd ridden in, prizes I'd

won, a commercial for cowboy hats that I did, and yes, people, too. Friends my brother tells me we spent time with I have no memory of having seen, people I'd just met, people I wish I hadn't forgotten.''

Willow didn't know exactly what that last part meant. "How could you wish you hadn't forgotten someone if you've forgotten them?''

"It's kind of like the way it was with Black Arrow. Almost like an itch I can't reach. Something tells me things were important, but I don't know why or what or who, and I just keep hoping something will happen to bring it all back. Or at least some of it.''

It was slowly sinking in that it wasn't only her and their night together that he didn't recall. That it wasn't a matter of her being unmemorable or of him having so many one-night stands that they didn't mean anything to him. She and their night together were a part of a bigger picture. A part of many things that he'd lost.

"So you actually have a medical condition?'' she asked, just to have it confirmed.

"A part of the memory portion of my brain was damaged from the concussion and induced a limited amnesia, yes. I know it sounds incredible, but that's what happened.''

I could tell him, Willow thought. *Right now. I could tell him he's already met me. On that Friday night before his accident. That we were together all night and that was where he heard about Black Arrow.*

But would that bring it all back to him? she wondered. Or would it only seem like a story to him? Maybe not even a believable one, since she hadn't mentioned it before now.

She had no way of knowing.

But what she might have was an opportunity, she thought suddenly. The opportunity to let him get to know her. The real her—Willow. Not the dressed-up, drinking, partying Wyla who had spent the night with him before she even knew him.

And if she used that opportunity to let him get to know the real her, maybe he would like her for who she was.

The idea appealed to her.

It was as if she could erase—at least temporarily— the one thing she'd done that she was most ashamed of. The one thing that gave the absolutely wrong impression of her and of the person she truly was.

It was almost like having a clean slate. For a little while, anyway. And at this point, she thought, she should take what she could get.

So she didn't tell him that she was one of the people he'd forgotten. That they'd spent the night together in Tulsa. She held her tongue and allowed herself to take advantage of an opportunity that maybe fate had offered her. Instead of telling him anything, she said, "Are the headaches from the concussion?"

"Yeah. The doctors say they'll probably go away eventually, and they are getting better. But still, when one hits, I'm in a world of hurt."

"I should go then, and let you rest. You're probably wiped out after you've had one."

"I'm fine," he assured her again.

But Willow was so relieved, so thrilled that she hadn't been just one of many unnoteworthy one-night stands that she almost felt giddy, and she was afraid it might show if she didn't get out of there.

So she set her glass on the floor, too, and stood. "No, really, I should be going." Then she screwed up her courage for the second time and said, "But if you want, we could do some furniture shopping tomorrow evening. After I close up the store."

He stood again, too, pausing to smile down at her as if he liked not only the suggestion, but what he saw, as well. And it did fluttery, feminine things to her insides.

"You'd do that for me?" he asked in a flirty tone she remembered well.

"Sure. Just consider me Black Arrow's welcoming committee," she flirted back, surprising herself by how easily she'd fallen into it.

"You wouldn't mind?"

She wouldn't have minded even if she didn't have a secret agenda. "No, honestly, I don't mind."

"That would be great, then. I really need a couple of tables—like a coffee table and maybe a kitchen table. I'm sick of standing at the counter to eat."

"Good. Then it's a date."

Why had she said that? She could have kicked herself.

"Not a date date," she amended in a rush. "I wasn't asking you out or anything. I mean I'm not coming on to—"

"I know," he said, stopping her before she made things any worse. Then he leaned slightly forward and confided, "It would have been okay even if you were."

Willow was not a person who blushed. She'd grown up with four brothers, after all. She would never have survived if she had been overly sensitive. But she could feel her cheeks heating and she didn't seem to be able to stop it.

And worse yet, she knew he was seeing it because his agile mouth stretched into an amused grin.

Unlike her brothers, he didn't say anything about it, however. "When's closing time? I'll meet you at your store."

"Six. Closing time is at six," she managed to reply.

"Maybe after we're finished shopping I could buy you dinner. As payment for your decorating services."

"You don't have to do that."

"How about if I just want to?" he said, a hint of a smile playing at the corners of his mouth.

"I guess that would be okay," Willow conceded. "Nice, even."

"Then it *is* a date."

He was teasing her. She could see it in the sparkle in his eyes. In that quirk of his lips that let her know he was enjoying himself.

And then, from out of nowhere, Willow had a burst

of memory from their night in Tulsa, and what hadn't been clear in her mind before—how she'd gotten from the blues club to his room—became vivid.

It had started with a kiss. A good-night kiss he'd asked if he could have when he'd walked her outside after the club had closed and they were facing each other just the way they were at this moment. A simple good-night kiss that had lit a fire between them and gone on from there.

And in that instant Willow wondered if, were he to kiss her now, it would be as combustible.

But of course, he wasn't going to kiss her.

She also knew it absolutely *shouldn't* happen, even if it were a possibility. That she shouldn't let it happen, since she was trying to amend the impression he would have of her if he could remember her.

But still she couldn't help wondering...

"I'd better go," she said more forcefully, heading for the front door. "Thanks for the tea."

"Thanks for bringing the papers out," he countered, following in her wake.

He reached the door in time to open it for her, and Willow went out onto the porch again, feeling oddly as if she'd just escaped something. Herself, probably.

"See you tomorrow," she said as she kept on going down the porch steps to her truck.

"I'll be there at six," he called after her.

Willow missed the door handle on her first try and had to make a second attempt, hoping he didn't realize why she was so flustered.

But it wasn't a good sign that he was grinning again.

Be cool, she advised. *Be cool.*

Because Wyla would never have blushed or flubbed opening the car door, and Willow didn't want to be a woman who did, either. She wanted to be smooth and self-confident and sure of herself, the way she had been that night in Tulsa.

The way she had been the first time Tyler had liked her.

That first time that he hadn't just forgotten, that he actually had a medical reason for not remembering.

Which meant that he wasn't a creep at all.

And that she wasn't necessarily forgettable, either.

Chapter Three

"Hey."

Willow looked up from the paperwork she was doing at her desk the next afternoon to see her oldest brother, Bram, standing in her office doorway.

"Hi," she replied, setting down her pencil.

"Got a minute to spare for your favorite brother?"

"Sure."

"I wanted to talk to you."

"I already told you I didn't rob that bank, Sheriff," she joked.

Bram came in, closing the door behind him. "Don't make fun," he ordered.

But Willow knew he was only kidding. She and the rest of her brothers were proud of the fact that Bram was Black Arrow's sheriff, and they'd made him aware of it.

Bram sat in one of the visitors chairs, leaned low in the seat and put his feet up on the corner of her desk.

"Anyone who puts their big clodhoppers up there has hell to pay with me," Willow warned.

Bram was unperturbed. "Don't make me come around there and give you a noogie to put you in your place."

Noogies were what her brothers called it when they put her in a headlock and rubbed their knuckles on her skull.

His threat must have been more effective than hers because he grinned and left his feet where they were, and Willow didn't do anything about it.

"Met Carl at the gas station last night," her brother said then.

"Uh-huh." Willow braced for what she knew was coming, since she'd already had this conversation with two of her other three brothers. Apparently Bram, Ashe and Logan had had breakfast this morning and discussed her, and if Jared hadn't married and moved to Texas with his new wife, he would have been in the mix, too.

"Carl says something's wrong with you," Bram continued. "He thinks you're sick or something."

"And you reported it to the other Musketeers over breakfast," Willow said. "Well, I'm not sick or anything. Just like I told Ashe and Logan when they called."

But Bram wasn't going to let it drop that easily. "Carl says he caught you sleeping at your desk. That you're dragging your tail around here, and that you don't even have the strength to move a feed sack."

Willow had made a special call to her doctor to ask if it was all right for her to go on lifting the heavy bags of feed and grain that she'd always hoisted without a second thought before. The doctor had advised against it.

"I have the strength. I'm just trying to learn to delegate."

Bram looked at her as if she were out of her mind.

"I know this comes as a surprise to you," Willow said, "but I'm not a man. And I might want to have kids someday. Gloria always said I shouldn't be lifting such heavy things or I was going to strain my insides, and I just thought maybe it was time to take that seriously."

Bram laughed. "Right. You're a delicate little daisy." He *was* making fun.

"I didn't say I was a delicate little daisy. But I'm also not one of the guys. And the guys around here can do the lifting. That's what I pay them for."

She hadn't intended for that to come out so brusquely, but it had, and she hoped her brother might just let it pass.

No such luck.

"Geez! Don't bite my head off," he exclaimed. "That's another thing Carl said—you're not acting like yourself. I can see what he means. Touchy, touchy."

Willow rolled her eyes.

"Carl says you're always in the bathroom, and the other day when he came looking for you he was pretty sure you were in there throwing up."

"Oh for crying out loud, I had the flu," Willow said, as if it were nothing. "And what's Carl doing counting how many times I'm in the bathroom?"

Bram ignored her question to ask one of his own. "Why didn't you call one of us if you were sick?"

"Because I'm a big girl and I can take care of myself," Willow said, exasperation ringing in her voice.

Her brother stared at her, his forehead creased in a frown, and Willow knew that she was not putting on a convincing defense.

She made a conscious effort to lighten her tone and said, "I appreciate that you care. You and the rest of the guys, and even Carl. But I can't call you all every time I have a hangnail. I must have caught a bug of some kind, which was here and gone before it was worth talking about."

"Are you sure?" Bram asked suspiciously.

"I'm positive. I'm fine." Then Willow decided the best thing to do was to get him talking about something else, so she said, "Is that the only reason you came in here today?"

"No. I was coming in to talk to you anyway, and then I met Carl and he gave me another reason."

"So what was the first reason?"

Bram went on staring at her for a moment longer, as if he wasn't sure he should let her throw him off track.

Willow calmly waited him out, afraid that any more attempts to defend herself would be overkill and do more harm than good.

Apparently it worked, because he finally said, "I wanted to know if you'd seen anyone suspicious hanging around, or if you've had anybody asking questions about us."

"Not that I know of. Why?"

"Some people say there's a tall, skinny guy—homely with dirty brown hair—asking questions about our family."

Willow shrugged. "That could be a lot of people we know. But no, I haven't seen anyone fitting that description who we *don't* know. Are you thinking this might be the same guy who broke into the newspaper office and set the fire at the town hall?"

Both were recent incidents that Willow knew Bram was investigating.

"Could be," he answered noncommittally. "The guy is asking about Gloria and any kids or grandkids she might have had. Which brings me to my next point—have you gone through her room yet like I asked you to?"

Bram had been after Willow to do that for weeks now, ever since he'd been contacted by another stranger in town. Rand Colton, a visitor from Washington, D.C., had brought up the possibility that there might be a connection between his family and theirs. It had become Willow's job to go through Gloria's things to find out if there was any information their grandmother might have had about it. Willow knew Bram was particularly curious because on her deathbed, Gloria had implored him to *find the truth,* something he was still trying to figure out the meaning to. She couldn't help wondering if this stranger had anything to do with that request.

"No, I haven't gone through her room yet," Willow admitted somewhat reluctantly. She was embarrassed at how long she'd been dragging her feet about it.

"I know it's a tough thing to do," Bram said, showing more understanding than he had about her not wanting to lift feed sacks. "Do you want me to do it?"

"No, I said I would and I will."

"When?"

"Tomorrow. I'll do it tomorrow," she promised, knowing herself well enough to know that if she made a firm commitment she would follow through even though it was something she didn't want to do.

Bram knew her, too, and didn't need any further assurance. "Good. You may not find anything important or revealing, but we need to rule out the possibility. And who knows? There might be something up there that will help me figure out what's going on."

Willow nodded in spite of the knot her stomach twisted into at the prospect of going into her grandmother's room, going through her things.

But her brother was satisfied.

Unfortunately, that meant he was ready to return to the previous subject.

"And you're sure you're okay?" he said.

"I'm sure. But if I come down with scurvy or rickets or green slime disease, you'll be the first to know," she joked, trying to cover up the uneasy feeling she had that her brother suspected the truth.

Bram gave her that hard stare again, but before it went on too long, there was a knock on the door. It opened at about the same time, and a strikingly pretty, blond-haired, blue-eyed head popped through the opening.

"It's just me."

"Me" was Jenna Elliot, and Willow saw her brother's whole being light up instantly.

"Come on in," Willow invited as Bram yanked his feet off her desk in a hurry and stood.

It didn't take a genius to see how much he cared for Jenna, who had nursed their grandmother after the first stroke Gloria had suffered in July and gotten involved with Bram in the process.

"I got your message to meet you here," Jenna said to Bram, her own face beaming with love for him in return.

To Willow, Bram said, "We're going for coffee. Want to come with us?"

Coffee was the one thing that could make Willow nauseous even after the morning sickness had passed. Even the thought of it raised her gorge.

"Thanks, but I have work I need to finish up. Besides, you know you don't want me horning in on you guys."

Neither of them denied it; they merely exchanged a glance that verified that they couldn't wait to be off alone.

But Jenna also seemed to have an attack of conscience about not really wanting Willow to tag along, because she said, "It seems like I haven't seen you forever, though, Will. Think we could have lunch? Maybe Saturday?"

"As a matter of fact I've hired a few high school kids to come in Saturdays now, so I probably can sneak away for lunch."

"Oh good. One o'clock at the coffee shop?"

"I'll be there."

Bram had stayed out of the exchange to that point. But then he said to Jenna, "Maybe you can get her to tell you what's going on with her."

"What's going on with you?" Jenna asked Willow, surprised.

"Nothing. Carl is imagining things and telling tales out of school about it."

Jenna looked from Willow to Bram, clearly confused and not thrilled at being put in the middle of whatever was going on between brother and sister.

"I'll fill you in over our coffee," Bram promised.

"There's nothing to fill in," Willow said.

But neither her brother nor her friend paid much attention to that.

Instead Bram placed a hand at the small of Jenna's back to steer her toward the door again. "Let me know if you find anything tomorrow," he said to Willow.

"I will."

"And I'll see you on Saturday," Jenna added.

"One o'clock at the coffee shop."

"See you later, delicate little daisy," Bram said then in a near singsong, referring back to his earlier remark about her not lifting grain sacks.

Willow just made a face at him as he ushered Jenna out of the office.

It was difficult for Willow to return to work, because she knew she was about to be the topic of conversation between her brother and her friend, and it wreaked havoc on her concentration. She couldn't help worrying that the more people thought about and talked about what was going on with her, the greater the chance that someone would guess her secret.

Willow took off work not long after Bram and Jenna left her office. She wanted to do some shopping for herself before her evening of furniture shopping with Tyler.

Ordinarily she bought most of her clothes out of catalogs, so the local boutique was not a place she frequented. In fact, her going into the place was such a change of pace that the owner and the clerk assumed she was there to buy a gift. Neither of them hid their shock very well when she informed them that she was looking for a few things for herself.

They recovered fairly quickly, though, and then pounced on her like hungry tigers attacking fresh meat.

Still, it served her purposes.

By the time Willow left she had several new outfits, with shoes to match. She also had chopsticklike things to put in her hair—if she could twist it up the way the salesgirl had shown her—plus mascara, blush and a lipstick that was not quite as dark as the one she'd worn in Tulsa, but a good color for her just the same.

She didn't even care that the clothes wouldn't fit soon and would probably be out of style when she could wear them again. She was only thinking of the here and now, and here and now she wanted a few things that would make her feel more like Wyla.

With bags in hand, she returned to the Feed and Grain, made sure everything was going smoothly, and went up to her apartment to change so she would be ready well in advance of six o'clock. She didn't want Tyler guessing that she'd done all this just for a simple evening of picking out tables. He might suspect how eager she was to see him again, and she definitely didn't want that.

She didn't even want to admit it to herself.

Truthfully, she didn't know what she hoped would come of this plan to let him get to know her. It wasn't as if she had some fantasy that he would spontaneously regain his memory, pull her into his arms and pledge his undying love for her on the spot.

She guessed what she was really after was just recollection, plus an amiable relationship with him, so that *then* she could make up her mind about whether or not to tell him he was going to be a father.

That seemed reasonable enough.

But if Tyler remembering her and feeling friendly toward her were all she wanted, why had she been counting the hours until she got to see him again? Why was her stomach aflutter at the simple prospect? Why had she bought a push-up bra, of all things?

Maybe it was just ego, she thought as she stepped out of her second shower of the day and dried off.

Certainly her ego had taken a hit when she realized that Tyler had forgotten her. And even now, knowing that a medical condition had caused his lapse in memory, there was still a residual bruise to her self-esteem.

It wasn't rational. But in spite of pointing out that irrationality to herself, in spite of telling herself she wasn't the only thing he'd forgotten, Willow still felt bad that he had forgotten her and that night in Tulsa. Somehow it seemed as if she and their night together should have made such an indelible impression that not even a concussion and a coma could have wiped them out.

So ego was probably at the root of her eagerness to see him again, she decided. Just plain ego. Which meant that she was more eager for him to see her than for her to see him, and not so attracted to him that she couldn't wait to be with him again.

"And you're a big fat liar," she said to her reflection in the mirror when she went to take stock of how she looked. She'd foregone wearing the push-up bra, but had put on a slightly low-cut, figure-hugging white V-neck T-shirt and the formfitting navy blue slacks she'd bought earlier.

Okay, so this whole mini-makeover and her eagerness to see Tyler again were not merely bandages to her self-esteem, she conceded as she delved into the mysteries of mascara and blush. She *was* attracted to the man. Why else would she have gotten carried away in Tulsa?

But it didn't mean anything. It didn't mean she thought they were going to end up together or anything. It didn't even mean that that was what she wanted.

It just meant that he was a terrific looking guy who made her feel like a woman.

Who made her feel like a woman...

That thought hung in her mind as if it had some special magic.

Was it also possible that feeling like a woman around Tyler Chadwick played a role in this whole eagerness thing?

Maybe.

And that possibility made something else occur to her.

Her great-grandfather, George WhiteBear—an old Native American who still practiced many of the old traditions—always claimed to have visions. And he'd told her not long ago that she would blossom and bloom during the brightest of midnights.

After finding out she was pregnant, she'd assumed

that the pregnancy was the blossoming and blooming. But now she wondered if it might have meant something else, too. If it might have meant that she would finally be blossoming and blooming into womanhood.

And maybe this whole thing with Tyler was a part of that. Maybe it was her first real chance to relinquish the tomboyishness that had been a natural result of growing up with four brothers. Maybe Tyler was giving her an excuse to finally step out into the world as a woman.

"Or maybe he just has the best face, body and butt you've ever seen," she exclaimed to her reflection in the mirror.

But as she ran a brush through her hair and carefully applied the new lipstick, she decided she was eager to see him for all those reasons.

Yes, Tyler Chadwick was a drop-dead gorgeous guy. Yes, he had a body to die for. Yes, she'd liked him in Tulsa and had been attracted enough to him to sleep with him.

But her ego had taken a blow when he hadn't remembered her—no matter what the reason—and she would like it if she could stir that memory.

And yes, it was time for her to break free of her tomboy persona and finally become the woman she was, too. It was probably long past time for that.

"I never thought furniture shopping could be so complicated," she said facetiously to herself.

But then, since meeting Tyler Chadwick, everything seemed to have gotten more complicated.

And she wasn't too sure if it would ever get uncomplicated again. In fact, she didn't know how it could when, in less than seven months, she would bring a baby into the picture.

But that prospect and the even greater complications it would bring were not things she could think about right now. So she put them on a back burner mentally.

No, right now she had enough to deal with—beginning with this evening. And that was what she had to focus on.

First things first.

So Willow took a deep breath and gave herself a final once-over in the mirror, deciding she hadn't done too bad a job at feminizing herself, while still maintaining a semblance of her own style.

And since that was the case, and she was determined to take things one step at a time, she slipped her feet into a pair of sandals and left her apartment, heading down the staircase that led into the store.

"Willow? Is that you?"

Carl was bringing a sack of chicken chow from the storeroom as she came down the steps.

"Of course it's me," she said, as if the question were ridiculous.

"Doesn't look like you," he countered.

"Good," she said defiantly, offering no explanations as she went straight to her office, hopefully to get the tension she was suddenly overwhelmed with to ease up before Tyler got there.

Tyler Chadwick who was only incidental to her

blossoming and blooming as a woman, she assured herself.

Although thinking of the incredible Tyler Chadwick as incidental to anything was a little hard to buy....

Willow was watching for Tyler when he walked through the Feed and Grain's front door.

Unfortunately, it was exactly when Carl was about to walk out of it.

"Sorry, Tyler, but we're closed. Can you come back tomorrow?" Carl said in greeting.

"That's okay. I'm not here to buy anything. I'm here for Willow," Tyler informed him matter-of-factly.

It gave Carl pause, though. He looked from Tyler to Willow, and then his eyes widened as if the light had just dawned.

And if Willow had had any hope of her brothers not finding out immediately that she was spending the evening with Tyler Chadwick, that hope flew out the window right then and there. She had no doubt that Bram would be hearing about this within the next fifteen minutes, and word would spread from there to her other brothers.

But somehow she didn't care.

One glance at Tyler made everything else seem to fade into unimportance. Even the tension she felt about being with him again, about the course she'd set for herself, about everything that was going on, took a back seat to how happy she was that this moment she'd thought so much about, looked so forward to, had arrived.

Carl muttered a simple, "Oh," in response to the news that Tyler was there to see Willow. "Well, have a nice evening," he added, then left. But not without another confused glance at Willow—a glance she ignored.

Then Carl was gone, and Tyler turned his full attention to her.

"Hi," he said with a mile-wide grin that convinced her he was genuinely glad to see her.

"Hi," Willow answered, her voice more breathy than she would have liked.

She was standing in front of the checkout counter, only a few feet from where he'd stopped just inside the door. So she had a clear view of him.

She couldn't be sure, but she thought he might have dressed up a little for tonight, too. He had on a sunny yellow Western shirt with the sleeves rolled up to his elbows, a pair of tan twill jeans that fit him just the way jeans were meant to, and cowboy boots that made him a full five inches taller than she was.

His hair was clean and spiky, his face was freshly shaved, and he smelled as wonderful as mountain air after a spring rain.

All in all it was a heady package, and for a long moment Willow just drank it in.

Much the way he seemed to be drinking in the sight of her.

"You look good tonight. Too good for furniture

shopping,'' he said then, the appreciation in his voice and in his expression crystal clear.

"Thank you," Willow murmured, fighting yet another of those rare blushes. But it pleased her no end that he'd noticed, that he liked what he saw, and that he was giving her a compliment any man might give a woman, and doing it without the shock Carl had shown. Without the shock her brothers would have shown if they'd been there.

But as much as it pleased her, it also embarrassed her. Wanting to get past it as soon as possible, she said, "How's your head?"

"Fine. No headaches today."

"So you're up for some shopping?"

"As soon as you can get away," Tyler confirmed.

"Oh, I can get away. I just need to lock the door when we leave."

"Great. Then let's do it."

A tiny shiver of remembered delight ran up her spine at the thought of "doing it" with him, and Willow was glad it was not a response he could see.

But thoughts like that were the last thing she needed, and she willed herself to keep her mind on the straight and narrow.

"We can walk just about everywhere, unless you don't feel like it," Willow said as Tyler opened the store's door again and waited for her to join him.

He chuckled slightly as she went out. "I'm fully recovered from the fall, if that's what you mean," he informed her. "I was pretty banged up for a while, but I'm known for bouncin' back fast. I just get these damn—uh, these headaches now and then, but it isn't as if I'm weak or anything.''

Willow shot him a glance as he followed her out onto the sidewalk, realizing that her comment had been silly. All anyone had to do was look at the hard muscles that bulged against his shirt, at the thick thighs encased in his pant legs, at the robust health that emanated from him, to know he was more than capable of walking miles.

''Okay, then we'll walk,'' she said simply.

''Good. And maybe after we do the shopping and have dinner, you can give me the nickel tour of Main Street. I was thinking that you were just the person to give me the ins and outs of how Black Arrow works.''

''Sure, I'd be happy to,'' she said, thrilled to know that he had thought of a way to prolong their time together before it had even begun.

The furniture store was only about three blocks farther down Main Street, and Willow and Tyler were the only customers when they got there.

As they shopped, they settled easily into a routine. Tyler told Willow in general terms what he needed— a coffee table, a kitchen set, a couple of chairs for his living room, and a desk and chair for his den—and then he basically left it to her to choose the pieces.

''This is what *I* like,'' she said at one point. ''But is it what *you* like?''

They were standing in front of a pair of overstuffed chairs upholstered in a light-brown fabric imprinted with a pattern that looked like duck feet, and she thought it would go well with his sofa.

Tyler only laughed at her question. "You're talking to a guy who went from home to hotel and motel rooms and a furnished apartment. If it doesn't have any stains or holes, it looks good to me."

"You're as bad as my brothers. They won't even pick out their own socks," Willow said, rolling her eyes.

But she made Tyler at least sit in the chairs before they were added to the order that was to be delivered to him the following day.

Closing time had come and gone when they finally finished, and Tyler left it to Willow to choose where to have dinner, too. But that wasn't because he didn't know anything about food. It was because, being new to town, he didn't know what their options were.

They ended up at the Pizza Parlor, a small restaurant complete with checkered tablecloths, candles in Chianti bottles and a jukebox that kept the noise level too high to talk about much more than what other restaurants and take-out places Tyler might want to try in the future.

It was dark when they'd polished off their pizza and stepped back out onto Main Street.

Streetlamps had come on to keep the town's primary thoroughfare brightly lit, and already there was a sleepy quality to Black Arrow.

Willow was glad that she and Tyler were nearly the only people on the street as they strolled along, so that

she could point out where Tyler would need to go to
renew his driver's license or to mail a package, where
to get the best deal on new tires for his truck or to
have his dry cleaning done.

She also peppered her advice with little details
about the owners and operators of the businesses
around town, including some tidbits of gossip.

And then they'd come full circle, back to the Feed
and Grain, and she discovered in herself a full-blown
disappointment that it brought the evening to a natural
conclusion.

"I'll take you home if you tell me where home is,"
Tyler offered when they approached the store.

Willow took a few more steps to the side of the old
wooden building and nodded in the direction of the
long stretch of stairs that ran up its side to the second
floor. "This is home, too. I live in the apartment upstairs," she informed him. Then, surprising herself,
she said, "Would you like to see it?"

The minute the words were out she doubted their
wisdom. But Tyler didn't hesitate to take her up on it.

"I probably should have checked it out before I
hired you on as my decorator," he teased. "But better
late than never."

Willow still wasn't sure this had been the best idea
as she led Tyler up the stairs, but she was so happy
he'd accepted the invitation that it didn't seem to make
any difference. She just kept thinking that maybe he'd
wanted the evening to go on a little longer, too, and
that that was a good sign.

Passing through the door from the outside landing put them in her kitchen—a big, warm country kitchen painted white, but accented in the colors of autumn, with a round pedestal table at its heart and four cane-back chairs pushed in around it.

"Would you like some coffee or tea or a drink or a soda?" she offered as Tyler came in behind her and closed the door.

"No, thanks. Just your company will be enough."

Willow wondered if simple, flirtatious statements like that gave other women the same warm rush they gave her. But one way or another his comment *did* give her a warm rush.

She just didn't know what to say in response, and that left her stammering slightly. "Oh. Okay. Well. As you can tell, this is the kitchen," she said, hating that she sounded so nervous. "And on the other side of that half counter is the living room. We can sit in there if you want."

"That'd be nice," he said, an edge of amusement in his tone.

He waited for her to lead the way into the other large, open room, and Willow did just that.

"There isn't much to see from here," she contin-ued. "Two bedrooms and a bath are through that arch-way. Well, two baths, actually. There's a tiny bath-room in my bedroom, but the main one is there in the hall. In case..." Was she actually suggesting he go to the bathroom? Tension had taken her too far.

But Tyler didn't seem to think anything of it. He

only glanced in that direction before taking in her russet-colored plaid sofa and matching love seat, her claw-footed oak coffee table, the oak entertainment center and the antique desk in the corner where the walls were wainscoted, paneled with tongue-and-groove pine and topped with a hand-carved chair rail.

"This is very homey," he concluded. "I like it."

Saved, Willow thought, putting some effort into regaining her composure. "It's small compared to your place, but it serves my purposes," she said.

"Do you have a roommate?"

"No. I moved in here with my grandmother a few years ago, but we lost her to a stroke last month."

"I'm sorry."

Willow nodded, appreciating his condolences. But her grandmother's death was not something she wanted to talk about, so she motioned toward the seating arrangement and said, "Why don't you make yourself comfortable."

He did, choosing the sofa, where he sat in the middle and rested both arms along the back. He also stretched out his long legs, crossing them at the ankles under the coffee table.

And Willow had the oddest urge to join him on that couch, to curl up like a cat against his side.

But she fought the urge and instead sat on the love seat, which stood at a ninety degree angle to the sofa.

"So how many of those brothers-who-don't-want-to-pick-out-their-own-socks are there?" Tyler asked then, referring to her earlier comment at the furniture store.

"Four. Bram, Jared, Ashe and Logan. Bram is the sheriff here, which is fitting, because he's always felt responsible for looking after and taking care of everyone. It's what he did—along with my grandmother and my great-grandfather—after our parents died."

And Willow wasn't sure why she'd offered so much information. Except that seeing Tyler there on her couch and feeling the stirrings she shouldn't be feeling were causing a renewed tension in her, and maybe she was overcompensating.

"When did your folks die?" Tyler asked, obviously unaware of the inner turmoil he was unwittingly causing her.

"When I was sixteen. In a plane crash."

"So you've lost your parents and now your grandmother, too. What about the great-grandfather you mentioned?"

"He's alive and well. Retired, of course, but we're lucky to still have him. He started the Feed and Grain originally."

"Does he live in Black Arrow?"

"He does. Not far from here. He'd never leave."

"Were you born and raised in Black Arrow, or did you come here after the plane crash?"

"My brothers and I were all born and raised here."

"And what gives you that incredible tan skin?" Tyler asked, studying her with an admiration that sent that warm rush through her a second time.

But she worked to ignore it and merely answered his question. "My skin color comes from Comanche blood on both sides of the family."

"So you're full-blooded Comanche?"

"No, my grandmother on my dad's side—the one who just passed away—married a Caucasian man. No one in the family ever met him, because my grandmother married him when she lived in Reno in her younger years, and he died shortly after. But he was white, which means my dad was half-Caucasian. So I'm not completely Native American."

"But enough to give you skin like smooth sandstone."

Skin that she could feel blushing yet again.

Maybe Tyler saw it, because he smiled a small, secret smile before he said, "And are all of these brothers of yours older?"

"All of them," Willow confirmed.

"How was that—growing up with four older brothers?" he asked, that secret smile broadening just enough to give a hint of that dimple in his left cheek.

"I think you're guessing how it was," she said, not intending it to sound so coy.

"I'm guessing it was tough. I know that if my brother and I had had a younger sister we would have teased her unmercifully."

"Unmercifully."

"And we would have been vigilant about keeping guys from coming anywhere near her."

"Vigilant."

Tyler's smile widened even more as he looked over both shoulders in mock fear. "So should I be worried about one of them popping out of the woodwork to scare me away?"

Willow laughed. "I wouldn't be surprised." Although it was on the tip of her tongue to say that her brothers had only ever scared away suitors, so if Tyler wasn't one of those, he was safe.

But she didn't say that, because she liked the allusion he'd made that a suitor was actually what he was.

Instead she said, "Carl is good friends with all of my brothers and has probably already alerted the troops that I was seeing you tonight. So, seriously, don't be shocked if one or more of them puts some effort into meeting you to check you out."

That was a friendly warning, just as she'd intended it to be. But Tyler didn't seem perturbed.

"Great. I'd like to meet them," was all he said.

"You might not feel that way once you do."

"Why? I like their sister. Why wouldn't I like them?"

That tripled the warm rush running through her. Especially since the comment wasn't offhand, but it was said with a bit of innuendo that made it carry more weight.

Still, Willow felt obliged to let him know what he might be in for. "My brothers can be pretty intimidating."

"More intimidating than a bucking bronco or a wild bull?"

"Maybe. You never had to ride four at once, did you?"

He laughed, still unfazed. "Are you telling me that you have four redneck brothers who might jump me for taking their sister out to dinner?"

"Well, only three of them are actually in town, and I wouldn't consider them rednecks, no. They'd never jump you, either. But like I said, don't be too shocked if the three who are around here arrange to cross your path."

"I think I can handle that."

But maybe he wasn't as sure as he sounded, because he chose that moment to stand and say, "I should probably call it a night now, though. It's getting late."

Willow felt a surge of disappointment. But she could hardly tell him she didn't want him to go, so she stood, too.

Tyler retraced his steps through the kitchen to the outside door, pausing once he had his hand on the knob. By then Willow had joined him to see him out.

But he didn't leave immediately. Instead he turned to look at her again. "So what do folks around here do for entertainment on Friday nights?" he asked.

Willow shrugged. "A couple of things. The movie house is usually busy. So is the Wild and Wooly— that's a bar that has live music on Friday and Saturday nights. Although more people go there on Saturday night than Friday. And now and then there's something else going on—for instance, maybe you didn't see the flyers up around town, but there's a carnival being set up about a mile outside the city limits. That'll be a big draw.''

''A carnival, huh? Would you care to go with me?''

Another woman would probably have seen that coming. But Willow hadn't. Particularly not when she'd thought the mention of her brothers had sent Tyler running like many before him.

''Are you asking me out on a date?'' she heard herself say before she realized she was going to.

''Why do you sound so surprised? That's what tonight felt like even if that isn't what you wanted to call it last night.''

She hadn't wanted to call tonight a date because she hadn't been too sure he'd go if she had. And because she wasn't altogether comfortable being the one to do the asking.

But this time she *wasn't* doing the asking. He was.

And she was entirely too happy about it.

She tried to keep her enthusiasm out of her voice. ''That would be nice,'' she said simply. ''But I can't promise my brothers won't be there.''

Tyler only smiled a confident smile and leaned slightly forward to confide, ''I'm okay with brothers. Even three or four of them.''

That made Willow smile, too. Probably more widely than she should have.

''All right.''

''I'll pick you up around eight—how's that?''

''Fine.''

Was she beaming? She felt as if she were. And nothing she did could keep that big grin off her face.

Except that suddenly something in the air between them changed, turning more intimate somehow. And Willow's grin relaxed as she began to think about kissing again.

Only unlike the previous evening, she was not thinking about what it had been like to have him kiss her in Tulsa that night in June.

She was thinking about Tyler kissing her now.

She was wanting Tyler to kiss her now.

She was thinking that maybe he was thinking and wanting the same thing...

On its own, her chin tilted slightly. On their own her eyes went to his. Warm, emerald-green eyes that seemed to wrap her in their gaze. That seemed to come a little closer. A little closer still.

And Willow waited.

She held her breath.

She felt as if her blood had stopped flowing in her veins.

She thought time might actually be standing still.

And she was so sure he was going to kiss her....

But he didn't.

He pulled back, stood straight again and said, "Thanks for your help with the furniture."

It took Willow a moment to come to her senses before she could grasp what he was saying, that he was saying anything at all and not kissing her.

But when she did she put a valiant effort into appearing as if she hadn't been anticipating more than that.

"I was happy to do it," she said, sounding overly bright, overly solicitous. Then she added, "Thanks for dinner."

"My pleasure," he responded, as if it really had been.

Again his eyes locked on to hers.

And again thoughts of him kissing her flashed through Willow's mind.

But only fleetingly, before Tyler glanced away and opened the door.

"Tomorrow night. Eight o'clock," he repeated.

"I'll be here."

"I'll be looking forward to it."

Then he said good-night and so did she, and he left.

And Willow felt considerably deflated as that disappointment that had begun when he'd started to leave grew to even greater proportions.

But it was for the best that he hadn't kissed her, she told herself.

She'd jumped into bed with him in Tulsa without a second thought, and jumping into anything else with him now was not what she wanted to do.

She wanted him to get to know the real Willow Colton, and the real Willow Colton would not have been falling into the arms of a man she'd just met, a man she'd asked out in the first place. A man she'd just gone shopping with, the way any two friends might.

"So it was for the best that he didn't kiss you," she said aloud, as if thinking it hadn't been enough to convince her, and maybe hearing it would be.

But it wasn't.

Because as she padded off to her bedroom, she still didn't feel convinced.

She just felt unkissed.

Chapter Four

Tyler's new furniture was delivered first thing the following morning, and by eleven he was sitting at his desk in the den trying to figure out how much feed to order from Willow.

But he was having trouble concentrating.

No matter how hard he tried, he just couldn't seem to keep his mind on Willow's feed. Instead, it was Willow herself he kept thinking about.

He'd had a great time with her the night before. And for him, having a great time shopping was nothing less than a miracle.

But actually, it had been Willow who had done the shopping, and he'd mostly just watched her. Which was why he'd had such a good time. ·

She'd taken pains to study each piece of furniture, and that had given him the chance to study her. To watch the signs of approval or disapproval, of pleasure or displeasure, play across that flawless face, brighten those dove-gray eyes, turn the corners of her full lips up or down.

That he'd liked.

He'd liked all the views of her as she'd taken in all the views of the furniture. The back view of that terrific tush, which had just the right amount of curve to it. The side view of breasts that were not too big, not too small. The full-on front view of long legs, curvy hips and narrow waist.

That he'd liked.

He'd also liked watching her try out the furniture. The way she'd sat so gingerly in one of the overstuffed chairs, then wiggled around a little until she was as cozy as she might be sitting in it on a cold winter's night in front of a fire.

He'd definitely liked that.

Oh, yeah, shopping with Willow was a whole lot better than shopping any other way he'd ever been shopping before. And it had set the stage for the rest of the evening. For dinner with her. For walking around town with her. For going up to her apartment with her. It had all been more fun because he'd been with her.

Because what he really liked was Willow.

And that was pretty much the rub.

He'd come to Black Arrow to find something he'd

lost—his mystery woman and the memories that went with her. And he wasn't doing that if he was with Willow.

Sure, he was getting out when he was with her. He was meeting other people, seeing faces in the distance—any one of whom might be the woman he was looking for, the woman who could jog his memory and bring everything back for him.

But the problem was that when he was with Willow he was *with* Willow. So completely that he wasn't thinking about anyone else, wasn't noticing anything else and certainly wasn't focusing elsewhere.

Which meant that, even if he *did* come across his mystery woman while he was out with Willow, his mystery woman might not register the way he hoped she would. The way she might if he came face-to-face with her *without* Willow.

So being out with Willow could actually be detrimental to his goal.

But still he'd asked to see her tonight.

Because there he'd been the night before, in Willow's living room, knowing it was getting late and he should leave, but not wanting to. Not wanting their time together to end. Not wanting to go without knowing when he might see her again.

And out had popped the words to make sure he *would* see her again. Tonight.

But ever since then he'd been wondering what the hell he was doing.

Spending time with Willow was time *not* spent

looking for his mystery woman. Which was the main reason he'd come to Black Arrow in the first place.

Plus he wasn't sure if he was being unfair to Willow when he was supposed to be looking for his mystery woman. When he hadn't given up the ghost of his mystery woman. When Willow didn't know there *was* a mystery woman...

Tyler raised his arms into the air and stretched until his back cracked, realizing he wasn't doing anything productive by staring at the figures he'd put on paper. Figures he wasn't even sure were right, since the entire time he'd been trying to work through them, his mind had been on other things.

Like the way Willow's coal-black hair fell around her shoulders in a silken curtain. Like how much he wanted to run his hands through that hair. How much he'd wanted to find out for himself if it felt as smooth and sleek as it looked. How much he'd wanted to play with it, bury his face in it....

Maybe his mind had been more than half on other things. Things like how much he'd wanted to cup her lovely face in his palms. To bring her closer. Close enough to get a better idea of how sweet she smelled. Close enough to kiss her good-night...

And what had he been doing, even considering kissing her good-night? he demanded of himself. If he was on the lookout for another woman he sure as hell shouldn't have been thinking about kissing Willow.

But that's what he'd been doing.

Thinking about it.

Wanting to do it...

Maybe that fall from the horse had knocked more screws loose than anyone had realized.

He wished his brother were there to talk it out with him. But not only was Brick *not* there, Tyler hadn't been able to get hold of him since he'd started trying early this morning.

But he knew even without talking to his brother that Brick would be glad to hear he was attracted to someone else. To someone in the here and now. Someone who was more than a memory he couldn't grasp.

Tyler knew his brother thought that trying to find his mystery woman was foolhardy. And he also knew that Brick was worried about the pull Tyler felt to someone he'd spent only one night with. Someone who hadn't left him so much as a phone number or an address where he could reach her again.

But Brick didn't understand the attraction Tyler felt. The pull he couldn't explain.

The draw, the pull that should have been keeping him from wanting to kiss Willow Colton and wasn't.

So what was he doing? Tyler asked himself. Juggling women? Because that wasn't something he'd ever done.

He knew guys—particularly guys on the rodeo circuit—who did that. Who never turned down a willing woman in any town they were in at any given time.

But that wasn't Tyler. Or Brick, for that matter. It was too complicated. Too dangerous. Too sleazy.

Yet here Tyler was, intent on finding one woman,

but spending time with an entirely different woman. Wasn't that sleazy?

But what was the alternative?

Either give up the quest for the mystery woman or give up seeing Willow.

Tyler shook his head. He couldn't give up his quest for the mystery woman. He had too many hopes that finding her would mean getting back his memory, too.

But he also couldn't stand the thought of not seeing Willow.

Which put him right back where he'd started: was he being fair to her?

He thought seriously about that. Very seriously, because he wanted to do right by her.

But the more he considered exactly what he was doing with Willow, the more he decided it wasn't altogether unfair to her. It wasn't as if they'd embarked on a grand romance or a serious involvement. They were just getting to know each other. And there was nothing fair or unfair about that. It wasn't as if he'd asked her for a commitment of some kind. It wasn't as if she couldn't be seeing other guys. And he *wasn't* seeing other women.

He was just looking for one.

Okay, no matter what kind of spin he put on it, it wasn't a really stellar thing to be doing.

But he had to do it.

Because at this point, he couldn't make himself give up either seeing Willow or keeping an eye out for the mystery woman.

But maybe what he could do, he decided, was be careful. And considerate of Willow's feelings.

He could work damn hard to make sure that things between them didn't go too far, while he tried to figure out who the mystery woman was.

But until he did, maybe he could just go with the flow.

He knew that would be what Brick would say. Brick would tell him to enjoy Willow, and if, in the process, he found the mystery woman, then just deal with that development when it happened.

If it happened.

And if it didn't happen?

Then maybe he wasn't meant to find the mystery woman again.

Coming to that conclusion on his own surprised Tyler, because it was the first time he'd seriously thought he might be okay with the possibility.

Which Brick would consider a step forward.

And maybe that was something.

Because it occurred to Tyler that while he still wanted to find the mystery woman, while he still hoped finding her would fill that gap in his memory, it didn't seem like the be-all and end-all the way it had before meeting Willow.

And that felt good. It felt freeing.

He just had to be extra cautious and not let that freedom go to his head.

Because what he wasn't free to do was hurt Willow.

Under any circumstances.

* * *

Willow knew it was irrational, but somehow she felt that as long as her grandmother's bedroom stayed intact and undisturbed, it was almost as if Gloria wasn't gone.

So in the weeks since her death, Willow had not so much as opened the door.

But now she had no choice. She'd promised Bram she would finally go through their grandmother's things, and that was what she had to do.

It wasn't easy.

Especially after a particularly bad morning of nausea.

Or maybe the nausea had been worse this morning because of the stress of knowing what she had to do today, what she'd begged off work in the store to do today.

Either way, as Willow stood at the entrance to her grandmother's bedroom, her stomach clenched. She could feel the tension in the back of her neck, and she suffered a fresh wave of shame, as if going into Gloria's former sanctuary would reveal to her grandmother what she'd done in Tulsa and the results of that rash act.

But Willow was resigned to the fact that she had to do it, so she took hold of the doorknob and went in.

The room was small and spare, and Willow was greeted with Gloria's scent—vanilla and lilacs.

That made it seem as if her grandmother was somehow with her, and suddenly not coming into this room, feeling ashamed of herself for the baby she was carrying, all seemed silly. As silly as it would have been not to confide in her grandmother if Gloria were still alive. Because in this room Willow felt the same kind of unconditional love, the same kind of warmth and acceptance she'd always had from her grandmother.

"Hi, Gloria," she said out loud, hearing the relief in her own voice. "I have to go through your stuff," she said then, as if her grandmother really were there and needed to be warned. "Those weird things that started happening just before your first stroke are still going on, and we need to figure out why. So Bram wants me to see if you left any clues in here."

It was odd, but having said that, Willow actually felt as if she had permission to do what she'd come for, and so she began.

The room held only a single bed, a night table, a few bookshelves and a dresser, plus an easy chair with a floor lamp behind it, where Gloria had liked to sit and read.

The dresser seemed like a good place to start, so that was where Willow went.

There was a gallery of framed family photographs on top of the bureau. Pictures of Gloria as a young woman with her twin sons—Trevor, who was Willow's father, and Willow's uncle Thomas.

There were also pictures of Willow's parents, of Uncle Thomas and Aunt Alice, of Willow and her brothers, and of all six of Thomas and Alice's kids, too. Plus there were photographs of Gloria's own parents—together when her mother was alive, and more recent ones of George alone.

It was a nice array, and even though Willow had seen them all more times than she could count, she still spent a few minutes looking at them before she started her search through the dresser drawers.

When nothing of any particular interest showed up there she moved on to the closet. Then the nightstand. Then the bookshelves. She looked under the bed and under the chair, and essentially left no stone unturned.

But two and a half hours later she didn't know anything more than she had initially.

She hated to call Bram and tell him that there was nothing among their grandmother's things that would explain why a stranger suddenly had an interest in them or why that stranger might have set fire to the town hall and broken into the newspaper office. But that seemed like what she'd come to.

Except that for no reason she understood, she felt as if she shouldn't rush into it. That she shouldn't give up yet, in spite of having searched the entire room.

She knew what her great-grandfather would say about it. He would say that Gloria herself was whispering to Willow's subconscious, telling her to keep going.

Willow just didn't know what else to do.

"So Gloria, if there's something in here we should know about, where is it?" she said aloud, thinking that her great-grandfather would be pleased that she believed in the spirit of her grandmother enough to talk to her.

And that was when Willow remembered something out of the blue.

She remembered her grandmother making a joke once or twice about hiding her fortune under her mattress.

Of course, no one had taken it seriously. They all knew Gloria didn't *have* a fortune.

But recalling her words, Willow began to wonder if maybe hiding things under the mattress had not been a joke, after all.

It probably had, she thought as she stood at the foot of the bed. But there was no harm in removing the quilt Gloria had made by hand. Or the blankets and sheets. No harm in turning the mattress just in case.

And that was where Willow found it—a lockbox tucked into a portion of the box springs that looked as if it had been cut away for just that purpose.

Willow hadn't come across any unaccounted-for keys, so she brought the box with her to the kitchen, where she used a hammer and screwdriver to break the lock.

And when she had, she found papers inside: a long letter and several documents.

A very important, very informative letter and very interesting documents.

Important enough, informative enough, interesting enough for Willow to make that call to her brother in a hurry.

* * *

Willow paced as Bram sat at her kitchen table and read what she'd found under Gloria's mattress forty-five minutes earlier. Each time she passed by him she tried to gauge his reaction, and she could tell he was as shocked as she had been.

"So it wasn't the way Gloria always claimed it was," Bram said when he finally finished the long letter and laid it on the table beside the documents, which included Gloria's marriage license and a deed to a property in Washington, D.C.

The letter was written to Gloria's sons. But it hadn't been in an envelope, and when Willow had unfolded the sheets, she'd realized at first glance that what her grandmother had written to her late father and her uncle was important enough to be read immediately. Even if it wasn't originally intended for her or for Bram.

"Gloria got married in Reno during that time she was there, hoping to break away from Black Arrow and her Comanche heritage," Willow said, as if her brother needed it explained. "But the Teddy Colton she married didn't die there shortly after the wedding and before anyone could meet him—the way she told everyone he had. They got married and had one night together, and then Gloria discovered the invitation to his wedding to another woman, and she left him sleeping in the hotel room. She thought he would come after her, tell her he loved her, and that of course he would break it off with the other woman. But instead he didn't come after her at all. He went ahead and married the other woman as planned.''

"Which makes him a bigamist.''

"And broke Gloria's heart. So she came back to Black Arrow. But it wasn't until she was home again that she realized she was pregnant," Willow continued.

"And when she *did* realize she was pregnant she hired a private investigator to find Teddy Colton to tell him?'' Bram muttered.

"Right.'' Willow confirmed it as if she were the expert, when in fact they were merely rehashing what had been in the letter they'd both read. "By then Teddy Colton had gone through with the second marriage, to this Kay person, and he didn't want anyone to know about Gloria or the pregnancy—which would have come out if he'd divorced Gloria and had to remarry Kay.''

"So instead he paid Gloria off.''

"By setting up a trust fund and signing over to her the deed to a piece of property in Washington, D.C. In Georgetown, specifically.''

"And the crux of it,'' Bram said, as if he were just seeing it for himself, "is that Dad and Uncle Thomas—''

"And all of us kids—''

"Are the legitimate heirs of Teddy Colton, while any kids or grandkids he had with Kay—''

"Might have thought they were the heirs, but aren't, because Teddy Colton's Reno wedding to Gloria was never dissolved. So his subsequent marriage to Kay wasn't legal or valid, and any kids or grandkids coming out of that union—''

"Are illegitimate," Bram concluded. "Wow."

"Wow is right," Willow agreed.

"Plus there's an inheritance," Bram said, as if the wheels of his brain were turning smoothly again after the shock of what he'd read in the letter. "And coincidentally, there's someone in town nosing around asking questions about us."

"Maybe part of the interest in us involves this deed," Willow suggested.

"I think it's possible," Bram agreed. Then, as if he'd just realized Willow was still pacing, he said, "Would you sit down? You're making me dizzy."

Willow did as he'd suggested, taking the chair across from him. "So what do you think is going on, Bram?"

"I'd say we've found proof of what Rand Colton was here looking for last month. That we *are* connected to this other branch of the Coltons. That we're the legitimate heirs of Teddy Colton. And that we seem to have inherited some sort of trust fund and some property in Georgetown."

"I meant does all this have anything to do with the fire and newspaper office break-in and this other supposed guy asking about us around town?"

"Maybe," her brother said noncommittally. "One thing is for sure, though—this could change some lives. Maybe lives of people who don't want them changed. Or it could take something away from some-one who doesn't want to lose it. Until we know exactly what's going on, I'm thinking that it would be a good idea for all of us to be a little extra careful."

"And to put these documents and the letter some-where safe," Willow added.

"After we show it to Uncle Thomas. Plus we'd bet-ter let all the grandchildren know, too, so they can be on guard in case there's any move made against any of us."

"Do you really think we're in danger?" Willow asked worriedly.

Bram shrugged. "I don't know, Will. I don't know what the D.C. property is worth or how much whoever wants it wants it—if that's what's going on here. I don't know what these other Coltons might be worried about losing to us, either. I do know that I'm taking the letter and the documents right now, showing it to Uncle Thomas and then locking it away at the bank so it's not here, putting you in possible jeopardy."

For once Willow was happy with the protective ten-dencies of one of her brothers. "You won't get any argument from me," she declared. "So, are you going to contact Rand Colton and see what he has to say about this?"

"He left me a few numbers where he could be reached. But I think first we'd better just let the im-mediate family know what's going on and find out who this guy is who's asking questions about us now.

And if he had anything to do with the break-in and the fire.''

''Do you have any other leads?''

''Not about anyone else who looks suspicious. But I have heard that there's someone staying in a trailer outside of town, and I'm about to check that out.''

Bram gathered up the deed and the pages of Gloria's letter to her sons, obviously preparing to leave.

As he did, Willow said, ''Do you think this is what Gloria meant just before she died when she told you to find the truth?''

''Could be. But she wrote the letter so long ago— right after Dad and Uncle Thomas were born, it looks like—that it's hard to know if there was something else she wanted uncovered. Something that's happened since then.''

''I think this is it,'' Willow said. ''I think when she realized Teddy Colton wasn't going to be a part of her life, or Dad's or Uncle Thomas's, she decided to keep all that a secret—to avoid the shame and humiliation. But she must have written the letter so that someday her sons would know what really went on. So they would know their complete heritage.''

''It's possible. But imagine making up that story about her husband dying.''

Willow had no problem imagining it. She knew exactly what it was like to get caught up in a moment the way the young Gloria had. To give in to an overwhelming spark of passion with a handsome, charming man who could sweep a woman off her feet.

And Willow also knew what it was to feel horrified by what she'd done when it was over. To worry about what kind of response she was going to meet from her family, her friends, her whole community when they learned she was going to be a single mother...

"Will? Are you okay? You're really pale all of a sudden."

Willow yanked herself back to the present and came up with a quick excuse. "I was busy going through things and I forgot to have lunch."

"Well, eat something now. I'd better get over to Uncle Thomas with this stuff so he can take a look at it before I have it locked up for safekeeping. Thanks for doing this."

"I'm just glad I found something. I didn't think I was going to."

Bram reminded her to keep her doors locked, said goodbye and left.

Willow stayed sitting at her kitchen table, still struck by the similarities between the path her grandmother's life had taken and the path hers had.

"So you really would understand," she whispered, feeling somehow comforted by the knowledge that she wasn't the only one who had gotten carried away by an overpowering attraction to a man and done something she would never have otherwise. Something she was embarrassed by. Something she'd paid dearly for.

But her grandmother had survived and ended up with two wonderful sons and eleven grandchildren who loved her.

"So maybe it will all work out for me, too," Willow said.

And in her hopes for that she remembered she had a date tonight with the overpoweringly attractive man who had gotten her into all this in the first place, and she still needed to shower, shampoo her hair and get dressed.

Which she headed to her own bedroom to do, feeling just a little less shame than she had before.

And hoping fervently that what she'd done in Tulsa in June didn't reverberate through generations the way her grandmother's night of passion seemed to have.

Chapter Five

Willow could already hear the carnival music playing in the distance when eight o'clock came and there were three sharp raps on her apartment door.

She didn't hesitate to open it. She was too excited at the prospect of seeing Tyler to prolong the anticipation any longer than necessary.

And there he stood, decked out and looking too good to believe.

Silver-toed snakeskin boots. Tight blue jeans and a belt with a World Champion buckle. A crisp white Western shirt detailed with blue-and-black points over each breast pocket. Spiky hair and a clean-shaven face.

"Hi," she said, with just a hint of awe in her voice as the scent of his aftershave wafted to her and she peered into eyes so green they hardly seemed real.

"Hi to you, too," he answered, taking a slow tour of her own sandals, navy-blue Capri pants, lighter blue tank top with bra straps, and hair twisted into the kind of knot the salesgirl had demonstrated the day before, held in place by the chopsticks.

When he'd taken full stock of Willow he said, "You look better every time I see you."

He had no way of knowing how unusual compliments like that were to her. Or how they turned her insides to mush.

Willow felt as if she were beaming again. "Thank you. You're not too shabby yourself."

That last part had sounded much more like what one of her brothers would have said than any way for a woman to compliment a man. She wished she could reclaim the words and think of something more feminine, more coy, to say.

But it was too late for that, so she opted for getting past her blunder, and said, "Would you like to come in or shall we just go?"

Tyler nodded over his shoulder in the direction of the carnival music. "Sounds like they've started without us. How 'bout we just go?"

Right answer. Because Willow was a little afraid that if she got him inside her apartment she might not want to leave again.

"Okay," she agreed, taking her keys and stepping out onto the landing beside Tyler.

"Shall we walk or drive?" he asked as he followed her down the wooden steps.

"I'm fine with walking if you are. It's only about a mile from here, on the edge of town. It'll only take us about twenty minutes to get there."

"Then let's do that."

They made small talk along the way, mainly about Tyler's new furniture—how it looked and if it worked for him.

Tyler assured her it was all perfect.

"I spent most of the day at my new desk," he said. "Not working, but trying to."

Willow was confused. "The desk was distracting?"

He leaned over to confide in her ear, "No, thinking about you was."

The devilish smile that went with the confidence sent small shivers of delight running up and down Willow's spine. But they'd reached the carnival by then, and Tyler stepped ahead of her to pay the entrance fee and buy tickets for the games and rides, so she had a moment to get some control over her response.

Which was a good thing, because she was worried she might be grinning like an idiot, and didn't want him to see it.

The carnival was a big draw not only for people from Black Arrow but for folks from surrounding communities. It pulled in so many people that the crowd was nearly shoulder to shoulder and the noise level was deafening.

Willow was only too happy to see the mass of humanity, though. It allowed her a degree of anonymity.

She saw people she knew and they saw her, but for the most part it was only to wave and holler a hello.

On the other hand, there were times when she caught sight of one of her brothers or cousins, and then she did her best to duck or to lure Tyler out of harm's way.

It didn't make for a relaxing evening, but she counted herself lucky each time she managed it.

And she was very lucky all evening, as she and Tyler rode the Ferris wheel and the merry-go-round and the Tilt-A-Whirl, as they went through the haunted house and the tent that displayed the two-headed snake, the biggest fruits and vegetables purportedly ever grown, and one of Elvis's guitars, among other novelties and oddities.

They also played chuck-a-luck. Tried their hand at the cakewalk. Threw baseballs at the paddle bar to try to drop the mayor into the four-foot pool of water he sat suspended over. And Tyler won Willow three stuffed animals and a bud vase by shooting wooden ducks with a pellet gun.

At ten the piped-in carnival music was turned off, and they wandered to the bandstand for the music competition. Groups and single singers, young and old, were competing for a first prize of fifty dollars. Willow knew some of them, but not all.

The acts varied from polka music to heavy metal and techno, and anything in between, including a girl who sang Patsy Cline songs almost as well as Patsy Cline herself.

Willow and Tyler both got into the spirit of the competition. At the end of each performance, they whistled and clapped and cheered, until the Patsy Cline singer was given first prize and sang one last song—"Sweet Dreams"—which the crowd was calling for.

By then the carnival was winding down, booths were closing, food vendors were cleaning up, and it was time to leave.

Even though Willow wasn't actually ready to call it a night with Tyler, they joined the stream of people leaving the carnival grounds, weaving among the cars and trucks parked beyond the entrance.

As they reached the first block of houses in town again, Willow spotted Bram. His patrol car was parked, blue and red lights flashing, near a car with what looked like a rental agency sticker on the bumper. He was standing with a man Willow had never seen before, studying his driver's license in the glow of a flashlight.

The man fit the description Bram had given her of whoever it was who'd been asking questions about them around town, and Willow felt a sudden sense of concern for her brother's safety rather than the desire to hide from him the way she had from her other brothers and cousins during the evening.

"That's Bram. My brother," she told Tyler.

"That's right, you said he was the sheriff. Looks like he's working tonight."

Willow couldn't merely walk on by, not after the

conversation she and Bram had had over the inheritance just hours before, and she came to a stop several feet away.

Tyler apparently noted her concern, because he said, "He seems to know what he's doing."

"For what usually goes on around here, he does. But there are some unusual things happening lately that we're thinking are aimed specifically at our family, and that guy looks like he might be the one Bram suspects of doing them."

"Don't you think your brother can handle him?"

"I suppose. I just can't keep from wondering if he really knows what he's facing, if that's the guy."

"It's probably not a good idea for us to distract him. But we can stay here and keep an eye on him if you want. Then if things look like they're getting out of hand, I can help him out. Would that make you feel better?"

"Yes, it would," Willow answered. And even though she never took her eyes off Bram and the stranger he was talking to, she mentally chalked up big points for Tyler for his kindness, his consideration, his sensitivity to her feelings.

She liked this man, she decided on the spot. And despite the consequences of what she'd done in Tulsa, at least she'd done it with a guy who seemed to be a genuinely nice person.

Just then Bram handed the stranger back his license, said something to him and then watched the man return to the rental car and leave.

Only then did Willow breathe easily again.

But once relief had settled in, she was left with a dilemma.

Particularly when Bram glanced her way and saw them.

There was no ducking out now. Bram would think that was strange, and no doubt so would Tyler.

But Willow would just about rather eat worms than introduce the two of them.

Then Tyler leaned over and murmured, "Shouldn't we say hello?"

Of course they *should*. But he didn't know what he was asking of her or what he was getting himself into. One of her brothers catching her out with a man? And her dressed…well, like a woman? This could be more trouble than the stranger, even if the stranger *was* the person who had set fire to the town hall and broken into the newspaper office.

But what could she say?

"I guess there doesn't seem to be any way out of it," she said in an unenthusiastic voice.

Bram waited for them to come to him, standing beside his patrol car, one fist on each hip and his eyes narrowing on Tyler as they approached.

"Hi." Willow greeted him without enthusiasm.

"Hey, Will," her brother answered, suspicion ringing in his tone as he looked from Tyler to her and back again.

"Tyler, this is my oldest brother, Bram. Bram, this

is Tyler Chadwick. He just moved into the old Harris place.''

Tyler held out his hand.

But Bram didn't rush to take it.

Willow had seen the tactic before. It was a way her brothers let someone she introduced to them know they weren't being immediately accepted, and that they'd better realize the fact.

Not until Tyler might have been considering withdrawing his hand, did Bram actually shake it.

"Tyler," he said.

"Nice to meet you," Tyler responded, in what surely must have been a lie.

"Been to the carnival?" Bram asked then, the question sounding as if it were for Willow, though his eyes were still leveled on Tyler.

"As a matter of fact, we were," Willow said, biting back a Sherlock Holmes gibe because she didn't want to make this situation worse than it was.

In fact, in an attempt to ease some of the tension in any way she could, she said, "That guy you were just with looked like the man you were talking about earlier. The one who's asking about us. Was that him?"

After another long moment, Bram finally took his sights off Tyler. But then, as if he were really seeing Willow for the first time, he didn't answer her question. Instead, surprise registered in the arch of his brows and the widening of his eyes.

"Well, look at you," he said, without any approval whatsoever in his tone.

And Willow suddenly felt as if she'd forgotten to put on any clothes at all.

But she wasn't about to let that show, so she said, "Thanks," purposely misconstruing the comment as a compliment, and pretending to take it in stride. She hoped Tyler wouldn't realize her brother couldn't believe she was dressed differently than Bram had ever seen her before. Plus she'd learned from experience that not making a big deal out of something one of her brothers was trying to goad her about was the best way to handle it.

Bram gave her the same hard stare he'd given Tyler, but Willow ignored it and reminded him of what she'd asked before. "The guy you had pulled over? Is he the stranger in town?"

Bram shot Tyler another sideways glance. "Apparently not the only one."

"Tyler isn't a stranger in town. He's a new resident. And the only thing he's been asking about is opening an account at the store."

"So you're the one Carl told me about. You and Willow had dinner last night, didn't you?"

"We did," Tyler confirmed readily. And to Willow's amazement he only sounded amused by this whole thing. He was completely undaunted by her brother. He stood his ground like a rock.

Which might or might not make things harder for him, Willow knew.

So once more she attempted to get her brother's

attention refocused. "The other guy, Bram," she reminded him a second time. "Who was he?"

After another pause, Bram slid his gaze back to her. "His name is Kenny Randolph. I was out looking for the trailer I'd heard someone was staying in, like I told you, and I spotted the rental car, too. He was just getting in it, so I thought I'd follow him, see what he was up to."

"And what was he up to?"

"Nothing much. He drove around awhile, then went to the carnival. I pulled him over when he came out, just to get his name. Now that I have it I'll check him out, see if he has a record. Probably put in a call to Rand Colton, see if he knows anything about him."

"So you do think he's the one who's been nosing around about us?"

"From the accounts I've had, I'd say he is, yeah."

"Did you ask him what he's doing in Black Arrow?"

"I did. He wasn't forthcoming. In fact, he has a smart mouth. He didn't answer me, just asked if it was a crime to stay around here."

"That was all you got out of him?"

"After some prodding he said that he was between jobs. Looking for work. I asked what kind of work he did, and all he said was 'this and that'—with an attitude. And you know there's all kinds of work around here now—farmers need hired hands for the harvest coming up. If the man truly wanted work, he'd have it. Plus he knows me by name. Seemed to want me to know that. Something is going on with him. I'd bet on it."

"But without much evidence from the break-in or the fire, you can't really connect him to them," Willow suggested.

"Or even bring him in for any serious questioning," Bram confirmed. "But I can keep an eye on him."

That last was said with a pointed glare at Tyler, obviously warning him that that was exactly what Bram intended to do to him, too.

But when Willow hazarded a glance at Tyler, she found him still unperturbed. In fact, his mouth was curved in a small smile that seemed to say *bring it on.*

And again Willow tried to distract her brother.

"Did you tell the rest of the family about the letter and the documents?" she asked, too desperate to consider if she should be mentioning them in front of Tyler.

"Yeah. And I showed them to Thomas," Bram answered.

"And then you took care of them?"

"Of the documents and the letter. Locked away safe and sound."

"And everyone knows to be careful?"

"Yep." Once more Bram aimed his gaze at Tyler. "They better."

Willow rolled her eyes, but neither of the men saw it because they were staring each other down.

"We'd better let you get back to work," she said to her brother then.

Tyler took her lead and said, "Glad we met."

"Uh-huh," Bram answered curtly. Dismissing Tyler by turning to Willow, he said, "Make sure *you're* careful, too."

"Don't worry about it."

"I do worry about you."

"Well, stop it."

Bram just shook his head.

Willow said good-night, then headed for the Feed and Grain again, Tyler at her side.

"So that's one of your brothers," he said when they were out of Bram's earshot, but still under his scrutiny as he watched them go.

"I told you my brothers could be intimidating."

Tyler grinned. "Who said I was intimidated?"

She had to admit that he hadn't seemed to be. Not in the slightest. "I'm just saying that..." She didn't know what she was saying, so she murmured, "I'm sorry that Bram wasn't friendlier."

"No big deal. If you were my sister I'd be doing the same thing."

Willow was inclined to point out that she *wasn't* his sister, though. Especially since she was a little worried that that might be how Tyler was thinking of her, since he hadn't so much as tried to hold her hand all evening. But she refrained, and just relaxed and enjoyed the comfortable, quiet walk with him.

She still didn't want to end their time together when they reached the Feed and Grain, so as they neared the outside staircase to her apartment she said, "I made some fresh lemonade today. Would you like a glass?''

"I would," he answered, as if he'd had no intention of calling it a night yet, anyway. "It's so nice out, why don't we have it sitting on the steps?"

"Okay," Willow agreed, liking that idea.

She had to make a pit stop in the bathroom again—one of many she'd made throughout the evening. She hoped he didn't know enough about pregnancy to guess that that was what was causing it. But whether he did or not, she wanted to be able to slip away without him knowing that's where she was headed, so she said, "Why don't you stay out here and enjoy the stars, and I'll pour the lemonade?"

"Okay," he echoed, and when they made it to the top of the stairs he sat down with his back resting against the railing.

"I'll just be a minute," Willow said as she let herself into the apartment.

Once there, she deposited the stuffed animals and the bud vase on the kitchen table, then she speeded through her bathroom visit and pouring the lemonade.

She managed to be back with Tyler within minutes, but even so the sight of him struck her anew, as if it had been months. His handsome features were bathed in milky moonlight, and she couldn't believe how terrific looking he was. Or that a man like him had been attracted to her once upon a time.

"Cheers," she said, after she'd handed him his lemonade and joined him on the top step.

"Cheers," he repeated, touching his glass to hers.

For once she was glad the landing was so narrow, because it allowed them to be separated by mere inches. And if he wasn't going to touch her—which she knew was for the best, but regretted just the same—at least she could be close enough to feel the power and presence that emanated from him.

"Tell me how you got to own the Feed and Grain," he said after he'd tasted his lemonade and judged it good.

"It's been in the family a long time. My great-grandfather started it and passed it down to my grandmother when he retired. I worked here as a teenager, then left for college in Tulsa, and when I came back, Gloria, my grandmother, passed the day-to-day operations over to me." After a sip of her own lemonade, Willow said, "What about you? How did you choose rodeo as a career?"

"Pretty much the way you ended up in the feed and grain business. My dad competed some and got my brother and me doing it early on. Not the bronc riding. He started us out with roping competitions mostly, calf roping as a team. Just being around the circuit put us on the sidelines watching the other events, and the older we got, the more we wanted to try our luck at it."

"And were you lucky at it? I mean, before the accident that ended things for you?"

"I'd say I was. It takes skill to compete, but it takes a lot of luck, too. It'd be hard to consider myself unlucky to have won three World Champion buckles in my career.''

"Three?'' she parroted, impressed.

"I was going for four when I got thrown.''

"It seems like a punishing way to make a living.'' Willow had been amazed by what a brutal beating most of the riders had taken at the rodeo she'd seen that day before she'd met him.

"It's a tough sport,'' Tyler conceded.

"Had you been hurt before that last fall that gave you amnesia?''

Tyler laughed. "Once or twice.''

"Meaning a lot.''

"I've had some broken bones. Some sprains. Some dislocated knees and shoulders and elbows. Goes with the territory.''

"Do you miss it?''

He laughed again, this time wryly. "So damn much I could spit. But I'll get over it. There're gettin' to be more and more redeeming qualities to being here, now.''

He said that pointedly, his eyes on her and a small smile on his face that sent a rain of something sparkly throughout her being.

Then he added, "For instance, I have a couple of apple trees right out my back door that I've never had before. And if I could find somebody with the know-how, I could have fresh apple pie one of these days, since they're chock-full of fruit.''

This time it was Willow who laughed. "Is that a hint?"

Tyler grinned. "It is if you can make pie."

"As a matter of fact I can. Crust and all."

"I'd do the picking and the peeling. And maybe even throw a couple of steaks on the barbecue that we could have before we eat the pie."

"Are you asking me to your place for dinner?"

He grinned a wickedly delicious grin. "Guess I am. Are you free tomorrow night?"

Willow was sure a more experienced woman would have played harder to get. But not only wasn't she that experienced, she was also pregnant. A pregnant woman who wanted nothing more than for the father of her baby to like her enough so that when she told him the news he wouldn't completely freak out.

"I'm free tomorrow night," she said.

"Think you'll feel like makin' a pie?"

"Maybe." That was as coy as Willow knew how to be. "As long as I don't have to climb a ladder and pick the apples first."

He nudged her shoulder with his own. "Why? Are you afraid of heights?"

"No, of ladders. I don't like ladders."

He laughed. "I promise I'll have all the apples picked by the time you get there."

"And peeled, don't forget. That was part of the deal. Then soak them in some apple juice in the refrigerator."

"Yes, ma'am."

With their plans for the next night firmly in place and the hour getting late and their lemonade long gone from glasses that had found their way to the landing behind them, that seemed to bring the evening to a close.

"I'd better take off and let you rest up for the pie baking," Tyler said then.

Willow didn't agree or disagree. She knew it was time for him to go. She just didn't want him to.

"Tonight was fun," Tyler added.

"For me, too."

"Thanks for the lemonade."

"Thanks for the carnival prizes."

"Sure," he said with another smile, but this one seemed so sexy Willow was hoping he didn't stand up right away and expect her to, too, because her knees were a little weak.

But he didn't stand up. He stayed where he was, looking into her face, into her eyes.

Willow didn't mind. She was enjoying the view of him too much herself. Of the carved planes of his oh-so-masculine face.

And suddenly she knew he was going to kiss her. She didn't know how she knew it, but she did. It was as if it was just in the air between them. The perfect way, the only way, to end this night.

Then he did. He leaned in and pressed his lips to hers in a kiss that was soft and sexy and all too short.

And when it was over, without moving away, he closed his eyes as if he were trying to distinguish a certain flavor, and in a low, intimate voice said, "Hmm. I've never kissed a boy, but I don't think that's what it's like."

"Excuse me?"

"Your brother called you Will—a boy's name. But you're definitely a girl."

Tyler opened his eyes and studied her face. "And you're too pretty to be a boy, too," he added. "Way, way too pretty."

Then he got to his feet in one lithe, graceful movement and went down the stairs with a bit of a hop to his step.

"Come out to the ranch whenever you're ready tomorrow," he said as he did, without looking back.

Then he reached the sidewalk and disappeared around the building.

And still Willow was sitting on the landing, feeling the heat that lingered on her mouth from his kiss, and the warmth that swelled inside her at the idea that he thought she was pretty.

Too pretty to be a boy.

Too pretty to be called Will.

And to her, at that moment, there were very few prizes in the world—carnival or otherwise—better than that.

Chapter Six

"Hey."

Willow looked up from reading her menu, surprised to see Bram at the restaurant the next day, when she was expecting the love of his life instead.

"Hi." Willow answered, with a question in her tone.

"Jenna had a home visit to do this morning and it's taking longer than she expected. She tried calling you at the store, but they said you'd already left, so she sent me to tell you she'll be here a little late," Bram explained as he pulled out the chair across from Willow and sat down.

"Okay."

Willow waited for the other shoe to drop. All morning at the store she'd been expecting her brother to show up, to talk about the previous night and meeting Tyler and what she was doing with him. She figured Bram had just been detained for some reason and had come to grill her now.

But that wasn't the topic he brought up.

"I've been looking into this Kenny Randolph character," he said instead.

Willow didn't breathe a sigh of relief. She knew that even if Tyler wasn't the first subject of conversation, her brother would get around to him. And even though she wanted to say *Oh, you're not fooling me, just get it over with,* she didn't.

She said, "Did you find out anything?"

"Randolph has a record. Mostly minor stuff in California. Petty theft. Vandalism. Two drunk-and-disorderlies."

"So he isn't an upstanding citizen."

"I could tell that just by his attitude toward me. But no, he isn't an upstanding citizen. I also called Rand Colton first thing this morning. He said he'd never heard of Kenny Randolph and didn't know anything about him. I wasn't sure I believed him until he offered to look into it himself, and called me back about half an hour ago. It seems that Kenny Randolph may have been hired by someone named Graham Colton."

"And Graham Colton is…?"

"Rand's uncle—one of two of Teddy Colton's sons by that Kay woman he was engaged to and ended up marrying after his fling with Gloria in Reno."

"The two sons who have thought all their lives they were legitimate and now find they aren't."

"Right. The two sons who also thought they were Teddy Colton's legal heirs up until now. Rand Colton says that's no big deal to his father, Joe, because he's made his own way just fine. But it's a different story with Graham. Rand didn't say anything against him, but he was hedging. He did say that Graham Colton always has money problems and that finding out he's not Teddy Colton's heir and that there's even one Colton holding—"

"The property in Washington, D.C.?"

"The property in Washington D.C." Bram nodded. "Anyways, Graham finding out he's not Teddy Colton's heir, and that there's even one Colton holding he won't have claim to, is likely a very big deal to Graham."

"A big enough deal to hire some thug to come here and ask questions about us and break into the newspaper office and set fire to the town hall?"

Bram shrugged. "Rand didn't state that outright, but like I said, he alluded to the possibility. He says the party line he tapped into revealed that Graham Colton just hired Randolph to disprove that we have any claim to anything. But you have to figure breaking into the newspaper office would have given whoever did it covert access to old newspapers that might have announced Gloria's wedding to Teddy Colton—something Graham Colton could be hoping isn't a matter of public knowledge. And a fire at the town hall could have destroyed Dad's and Uncle Thomas's original birth certificates—''

''And the main proof that they were Teddy Colton's sons and therefore his legal heirs.''

''Exactly.''

''Is this Washington property so valuable it's worth going to all this trouble?'' Willow asked.

''Your guess is as good as mine. But it's something else we should find out. For now, though, I'm more concerned with this Kenny Randolph guy. And you.''

Here it comes, Willow thought, convinced her brother was changing the subject to Tyler.

But again she was mistaken.

''I don't know how, but word has leaked out around town that you found proof of an inheritance,'' Bram said.

It took Willow a moment to realize they were still talking about family matters and hadn't switched to Tyler, after all. But when she did realize it, she said, ''The gossip is spreading already?''

''Somebody must have overheard something somewhere along the line. I warned the family to keep it under their hats, and I doubt if any of them let this out—''

''But maybe someone got wind of it at the bank when you had the papers locked up,'' Willow postulated.

''That's what I'm figuring, too. Anyway, however it happened, two separate people have asked me about the inheritance this morning and mentioned you in the process, and the fact that you found it in Gloria's things in the apartment.''

"Great," Willow said facetiously.

"Yeah. So I was thinking maybe you ought to come out to my place and stay until I get this whole thing under some kind of control.''

Willow appreciated his concern. But she wasn't about to do that. Her pregnancy wouldn't be a secret for long if she were in close proximity to her brother every morning. Besides the fact that there would be no way she could see Tyler or make any headway with him.

"Thanks, but I'll be all right at the apartment," she said. "I'll just be careful.''

Bram scowled at her disapprovingly. "I knew you wouldn't listen to reason.''

"There's no *reason* to believe Randolph will even be privy to town gossip, or that he'll think I still have the letter and the documents if he is. I'll be careful, but I'm not going to let the possibility drive me out of my home.''

"I'm trying to keep tabs on Randolph, but I don't have the manpower to watch his every move. It would be a lot easier if you'd just agree to get out of harm's way.''

"I'm not in harm's way. If it was someone at the bank who found all this out and spread the word, then they've probably also spread the word that the papers are all locked up tight in the vault and nowhere near me or the apartment anymore.''

"I made that clear to the folks I talked to this morning, but that isn't the juiciest part of the story, Willow. It may not be repeated."

"I'll be fine," she reiterated. "I jammed chairs under the doorknobs last night before I went to bed, and I'll keep doing that. But I'm not leaving the apartment."

Bram gave her a hard stare, as if that might change her mind. But Willow held her ground.

"Lord, you're stubborn," he said after a moment.

"I had some good teachers."

A small silence fell then and Willow was sure Bram was finally going to bring up Tyler, so she braced herself.

But he merely got up from the table.

"Here comes Jenna," he said with a nod toward the restaurant door. "I'll leave you two to your lunch. But be careful, Will. I mean it."

"I will," she assured him, stunned that he was leaving without so much as a mention of the night before or of Tyler.

How could that be?

But that's the way it was, because her brother headed for the door to meet Jenna as she came in. He exchanged a few words with her, touched her hand and gave her a small kiss before continuing on outside, as if the previous evening had never happened.

"I'm so sorry I'm late," Jenna said in greeting as she took the chair Bram had just vacated.

Willow was a little slow on the uptake, wondering

what her brother had up his sleeve. But then she said, "It's okay. Bram was just filling me in on this whole Colton-heirs thing."

"He's worried about you," Jenna said.

"I know. But I'll be fine."

Their waitress was a teenage girl they both knew well, and after asking about her family, Jenna ordered the tuna melt special.

Willow ordered a bowl of soup and prayed the smell of tuna fish from across the table wouldn't set off her stomach again.

"What's this I hear about you and the new guy in town?" Jenna said when the waitress had left them alone.

So that was why Bram hadn't said anything about Tyler. He'd sent Jenna to do it, probably figuring Willow would be more candid with her.

"What are you hearing?" Willow asked, debating about whether or not to be honest with Jenna. On the one hand Jenna was her best friend and she was dying to tell her everything. On the other hand, Jenna was seriously involved with Bram and might relay it all to him. And that was something Willow couldn't have happen.

"I heard you were picking out furniture with him the night before last, and Bram said you were together after the carnival last night."

Both things were true and had been witnessed by other people. Willow could hardly deny them, so she acted as if it was no big deal. "Sounds like you heard right.'' But she knew that had seemed too defensive, and resolved to curb her tone.

"I understand his name is Tyler," Jenna said, like a teenager hungry for information about her friend's juicy new romance.

"That's right. Tyler Chadwick. He bought the old Harris place."

"And is it a coincidence that he was a rodeo rider in Tulsa in June, and that you had a fling with a rodeo rider in Tulsa in June?"

Maybe it was better to have friends who *didn't* listen to what she said.

Not long after that night in Tulsa, Willow had complained to Jenna that she was smothering under the overprotectiveness of her brothers. Jenna had suggested she break free a little, that she go a little wild, and Willow had confided that she already had. But she hadn't given Jenna any details. Or any idea of the consequences of that night. She'd only said she'd already gone a little wild. With a rodeo rider. In Tulsa. In June.

"How did you know Tyler was a rodeo rider?" Willow asked, rather than answering her friend's question.

Jenna made a face. "Don't get mad, but since Bram heard you were with him at the furniture store the other night he's been asking around about him."

"Uh-huh." No surprise there.

"I didn't tell him that you had had a fling with a rodeo rider, or where or when, so you don't have to worry that I've blown your cover—if you have a cover. But I *have* to know—*is* it just an incredible coincidence?'' Jenna persisted.

Willow still wasn't sure how much to let her friend in on.

But wanting to tell someone something got the better of her. Willow segued into the topic by saying, "I don't want Bram or the rest of my brothers doing their usual routine."

"And scaring the guy off. I don't blame you."

"If I tell you, you have to promise me you won't tell Bram. Under any circumstances."

"Hey, I'm on your side when it comes to this. Your brothers, Bram included, are big pains in the neck about you having a life of your own. Especially a life that involves the opposite sex. And I know it. I've already gone round and round with Bram about this new guy. Bram wanted to get your brothers together and go have a talk with him first thing this morning, and I wouldn't let him. I didn't even let him call your other brothers about it, and I threatened him with extinction if he so much as said a contrary word to you about this."

So Bram hadn't said anything at all.

"You can tell me anything," Jenna continued. "I won't let out even a nugget of it to incite your big lug siblings."

Their lunches were served then, allowing Willow a moment to consider what her friend had said.

She knew Jenna well enough to know she wouldn't

be playing secret spy for Willow's brothers even if she *was* in love with one of them.

But still, once their waitress had left them alone again, Willow said, "You'd have to give me your solemn oath not to repeat anything I told you. I know my brothers, and just my being interested in a man is always disastrous."

"I'll go you one better. Not only will I keep any information to myself, but I'll try to convince Bram that you're just showing a new customer around a little. That it's good business. And if necessary, I'll keep him in line by threatening him again."

Still Willow hesitated, concerned about Jenna's connection to Bram. But in the end she decided that she didn't necessarily have to tell Jenna *everything*, but maybe it would be all right to tell her a little.

"I'm trusting you," Willow warned.

"You can," Jenna assured her.

"Okay, then yes, Tyler is the guy I met in Tulsa in June."

"And he moved here to be with you?"

"Not exactly." Willow tasted her soup and tried not to breathe too deeply as the odor of warm tuna fish wafted to her. "He doesn't even remember me," she confessed.

Jenna stopped short of raising half her sandwich to her mouth, and her expression reflected both curiosity and alarm. "He doesn't remember you?"

"I know. It sounds bad, doesn't it? But there's actually a medical explanation for it.'' Willow told her about the rodeo accident and Tyler's amnesia.

''I know from a neuropsychology class I took in nursing school that the memory functions of the brain can be complicated. Does he have any other problems that way?'' her friend asked worriedly.

''I don't think so. I believe the only other problem he has is that he gets really severe headaches.''

Jenna frowned once more. ''So you met him in Tulsa and had your fling with him, and now he's moved to Black Arrow and you're seeing him again, but he doesn't know he even met you before, let alone that the two of you had a fling in Tulsa?''

''Right. And I'm kind of glad he doesn't.''

''Why?'' It sounded as if Jenna really couldn't believe that.

''Because in Tulsa he didn't even know my right name. Becky has always called me Wyla, and that was how she introduced me to Tyler. And that night *Wyla* was a whole lot different than the real me. I decided that if Tyler can't remember *Wyla* I might as well use that to my advantage and see if I can get him to like Willow.''

''So you do want him to like you?''

''Well, yeah.''

What Willow didn't want was to look at the oil that glistened on the surface of the melted cheese that dripped out of the side of that tuna sandwich, and when she did she felt her stomach do its now-familiar lurch.

She took a long drink of water to wash back her gorge and raised her gaze to Jenna's face again.

But this time Jenna's expression was different. This time Willow had the sense that her friend had realized more than she wanted her to.

"Are you okay?" Jenna asked, sounding more like a nurse now than a friend.

"Sure."

"You don't look well all of a sudden. Is something about this food bothering you?"

"Tuna. I'm not big on it."

"Since when? I've seen you eat tuna before."

"The soup is good, though," Willow said, rather than answer Jenna's question. "Want a bite?"

"No, thanks."

Instead Jenna studied her intently for a moment before she said, "Carl has been reporting to Bram that he thinks something's wrong with your health."

"So I hear," Willow said, as if it were ridiculous.

"And Bram said you told him you'd had a touch of the flu. I was going to ask you about that. But now that I think about what Carl told Bram…"

Time seemed to stand still for Willow. Not only was Jenna a woman, but she was a nurse, too. She was trained to pay attention to symptoms and what they meant. And Willow suddenly felt as if she had Pregnant written in neon across her forehead.

Maybe she wasn't too far off, because Jenna's eyes widened to the size of saucers and she leaned across the table to whisper, "Are you pregnant?"

Willow didn't know what to do. She was torn between panic that her secret was out even to that extent, and the deep need to not carry that secret alone anymore.

And given that and the fact that she'd already trusted Jenna as far as she had, she finally went the rest of the way and nodded her head. Just once. And almost imperceptibly.

"Oh, wow," Jenna breathed. "And this guy is the fa—"

"Shh!" Willow glanced covertly from side to side to make sure no one might have overheard. Then she stared hard at Jenna and said, "Remember, you promised. You can't tell *anyone*."

"I know. I won't. But Willow…"

"I know. It's a mess."

"And he doesn't remember…anything?"

"Nothing."

It seemed to take Jenna a moment to digest this news and its repercussions, because she just stared into the distance with a perplexed expression on her face. Then she refocused her attention on Willow.

"Are you hoping that spending time with him will make him remember you?"

Jenna had always been very perceptive. "Eventually, yes, that would probably help."

"*Probably* help?"

"Okay, it would help a lot. But since things are the way they are now, I'd rather he didn't remember me right away. At least not before he's gotten to know me as myself.''

Jenna's brow wrinkled in bewilderment. ''This really is—''

''A mess. I know it only too well. I'm just trying to work it out.''

''Do you think he likes you? The way he did in Tulsa?''

Willow shrugged. ''I made the first couple of moves—I personally delivered his credit account acceptance and volunteered to help him pick out furniture. But it was his idea to go out last night. And tonight I'm going to his house for dinner—his idea, too.''

''That's good. And have there been any more… flings?''

''No,'' Willow said, as if it were the furthest thing from her mind when, in fact, each night since Tyler had walked back into her life she'd tossed and turned with the craving to do just that. And it certainly wasn't getting easier since he'd kissed her. The kiss had been like a sample to whet the appetite, leaving her wanting so much more…

''Since you've been spending this time together has he seemed to remember you at all?'' Jenna asked, breaking into Willow's wandering thoughts.

She shook her head. ''No.''

''What if he never does? Will you tell him? About Tulsa and about this?'' Jenna's eyes dropped to Willow's waist.

"I don't know. I'm just playing everything by ear right now."

"What about the *baby?*" Jenna only mouthed the last word.

"What about it?"

"Do you want it? Are you prepared to raise it alone?"

"Yes, I want it. It was a huge shock, of course. And at first I was just freaked out. But when I got a little more used to the idea I knew I couldn't do anything else."

"And if you have to raise it alone?" Jenna repeated.

Willow's stomach lurched again, but this time nausea and tuna melts had nothing to do with it. "I guess that's what I'll do."

"Do you *want* this guy to offer to marry you?"

"Oh, I don't know about that," Willow said quickly, her tone edged with panic at just the thought. "Right now I'm only thinking about getting to a point where maybe I can tell Tyler. If I decide I want to. I haven't thought beyond that." Which was true. It was all too easy to think beyond the simple kiss they'd shared since he'd been in Black Arrow. But to think beyond telling him they'd met in Tulsa and that as a result of it she was pregnant? That was a leap too big for her to make just yet.

"And your brothers," Jenna said ominously, as if she'd just remembered that complication.

"My brothers," Willow echoed, with an equal dose of dread.

"That could be bad."

"There's no *could be* about it. It *will* be bad."

The look on Jenna's face let Willow know her friend agreed. "I'll do whatever I can with Bram," she offered, but she didn't sound convinced that anything she might do would help.

"Thanks. But remember, for now he can't know anything. Not *anything.*"

"Don't worry, I know that. This Tyler guy might not live through the wrath of the Colton brothers if they knew what was really going on. And we want to give him at least the chance to step up and do the right thing. If that's what you want," Jenna was quick to add. "But no matter what, you know I'll do whatever I can to help if you need me."

"Thanks," Willow said again, hoping she wouldn't need her friend's help and that everything would work itself out.

One way or another.

Chris Isaak music was playing again when Willow arrived at Tyler's place after work that evening. After work and a quick dash up to her apartment to shower and change her clothes.

Willow could see Tyler coming down the stairs inside just as she was climbing the porch steps, since the front door was open and she could see through the screen. Bare feet first. Big, perfectly arched feet that turned out slightly and seemed more intimate a sight than she should be having of him in spite of what they'd shared two months before.

Then came his long, jean-clad legs and hips, and more skin. He didn't have a shirt on! Willow's mouth went instantly dry at the view of his flat stomach rising into the broad V of his muscular chest and shoulders.

"Hi," she said in a hurry when he neared the bottom step. His head was down as he dried his hair with a towel, so he hadn't seen her. But she was afraid that might change in an instant and he'd catch her gawking at him.

Up came his chin at the sound of her voice. His hands stopped rubbing abruptly, and the surprise on his handsome, whisker-shadowed face was replaced with a smile that radiated pleasure, without a bit of embarrassment that he'd been found half-dressed.

"There's my traveling pie maker!" he said with a grin as he came to the screen.

"I was just about to knock."

"I probably wouldn't have heard it over the music, anyway. Come on in," he invited, pushing the screen open for her.

He smelled of soap and shampoo as she passed in front of him, carrying the paper grocery sack full of the things she needed for the pie.

"Am I too early?" she asked.

"Nah. I'm running late. Once I got started picking fruit I hated to stop. I haven't even done any peeling yet, but I thought I could do that while you put the crust together or whatever you do before you need the apples.''

''Okay.''

He had draped the towel around his neck and was hanging on to the ends with each hand before he remembered his manners. ''Here, what was I thinkin'. Let me take that bag,'' he said, reaching for it.

''It isn't heavy,'' Willow assured him.

But he took it anyway, indulging in a long look at her when he had.

''I feel ashamed to have you baking pie lookin' so good,'' he said then, referring to the light-blue sundress she had on.

Willow had worried that it might be not quite right for what they had planned. But knowing she wouldn't be seeing anyone else—especially her brothers—had made her feel more free to wear the first dress she'd worn in Black Arrow since the Easter Sunday she was eleven.

''It's cool. I thought that would be a good idea if I was going to be in the kitchen with the oven on on a ninety-degree day.''

''Makes sense to me,'' he said with a slight nod of his handsome head.

Then, after another moment of gazing at her appreciatively, he seemed to notice the music that was still blaring.

''Let me turn this down.''

He went into the living room, taking the sack with him, and lowered the volume on his stereo.

"I like Chris Isaak, too," Willow said when she'd followed him into the other room and the sound was low enough for him to hear her.

"I was actually never a big fan before, but something about it since the accident has been so appealing I play it all the time now."

That struck a note with Willow. The night they'd spent together in Tulsa, Chris Isaak music had been playing loudly enough in the room next door for them to hear it through the walls. Willow had thought of it as wonderful background music. But when she'd heard it coming from Tyler's stereo the other day, it hadn't occurred to her that somewhere in Tyler's subconscious he might be connecting the music to their night together.

To her, maybe.

And if he was, then his newfound fondness for it was a positive sign....

"Want to get to work, or sit and enjoy the music until I finish shaving and dressing?" he asked then.

"I can get to work."

"You're the boss," he assured her, pointing his chin in the direction of the kitchen.

Willow led the way, finding a whole bushel of apples waiting for her on the kitchen table she'd helped him choose.

"I don't think we need quite this many," she informed him with a laugh.

"I was thinking you might want to take the rest home. Pass them out to your friends or customers or something. I have about twenty more bushels in the barn that I don't know what I'm going to do with, and there's still more on the trees.''

"Mrs. Harris was known for her apple everythings—pies, bread, cakes, butter, sauce. I guess now we know why.''

"Maybe I'll have to see if I can get them sold at the grocery store.''

Tyler put the bag on the table and lowered the bushel basket to one of the four kitchen chairs. As he did, Willow was treated to the tensing muscles of his incredible naked back. It sent a ripple of something sensual and very feminine through her, and she recalled Jenna's question at lunch about whether they'd had any more *flings*. Willow wanted to have one right now!

But she tamped down the idea and dragged her eyes upward just as he turned to face her again.

"Can I get you a glass of iced tea to start?''

"Iced tea sounds good. But why don't you go on with what you need to do and I'll pour it myself?'' Because the sooner he put on a shirt, the better.

"If you're sure,'' he agreed. "Glasses are in the cupboard above and to the left of the sink. Tea's in the fridge. You can pour two glasses and I'll be back before the ice melts.''

"Okay.'' And maybe in the meantime she could get herself under control.

He had to pass by her to leave the kitchen and as he did he paused to give her the once-over again, this time giving some extra study to her hair. She'd pulled it into a clip at her crown to keep it out of her face, out of the pie, and to keep her neck cool.

Tyler seemed to like it, because he tweaked a curl and murmured, "I'm glad you're here."

Then he impulsively kissed her bare shoulder.

The sensual ripple of moments before turned all glittery and gold, and left Willow in a haze of delight as Tyler left the kitchen.

"Get a grip," she muttered to herself when she was alone. Moving to the cupboard, she found two glasses, then headed to the refrigerator for iced tea.

True to his word, Tyler was back again while cubes still bobbed in his glass. His clean hair was freshly spiked; his face was free of five o'clock shadow. He had on a white T-shirt tucked into his jeans, and a hint of aftershave added a heady sensuousness to the previous scent of soap and shampoo.

But Willow reminded herself that being seduced by the way he looked and the way he smelled was not on tonight's agenda, and she tried to ignore the effects he was having on her.

She had begun to cut butter into the flour when Tyler joined her at the table to peel the apples.

They worked well together, exchanging small talk as they got the pie together and into the oven. Then they put steaks on the barbecue in the backyard and tossed a salad to go with them.

Willow was mildly surprised by how smoothly it all went. By how easily they settled into compatible con-

versation about Black Arrow and its citizens, about
apples and trees and Tyler's plans for herding cattle
rather than horses, about starting up a small dairy and
having his brother join him in business when Brick
was ready to leave rodeoing behind, too.

Before she knew it, dinner was done, the mess was
cleaned and they'd eaten pie—only one slice for her
but two for Tyler—and he was suggesting they sit on
the porch to watch the sunset.

Willow didn't have to think twice about accepting,
because she was nowhere near ready to say good-night
to him. Instead she agreed that sounded like a good
idea, and out they went onto the porch.

There was a single chair she could have chosen to
sit on, but instead she went directly to the porch swing,
which hung by chains from the roof above.

She didn't know whether Tyler would join her there
or not, and decided it was probably better if he didn't,
because as the evening progressed she was finding him
more and more appealing, more and more attractive,
more and more irresistible.

But when he did join her on the swing—sitting
close enough to her that his thigh ran the length of
hers—she was inordinately pleased.

They were just in time, too, because the sun was
setting in a mellow, cotton-candy glow.

They watched in relative silence, and that was nice,
too. But when full darkness had fallen Willow began
to wonder if she should say good-night and go home
then. Even though she still didn't want to.

Maybe Tyler read her mind, because just as she was about to suggest it he angled himself in the swing so he could look at her, leaving an arm along the swing back so he could fiddle with a strand of her hair. And any notion she'd had of ending the evening was chased away.

"If you listen real close you'll hear the symphony that came with this place," he said then.

"You have your own private symphony?" Willow asked, playing along.

"Yes, ma'am. Ducks in the mornings and frogs in the evenings. Listen."

Willow had been so intent on the sunset, on having Tyler close beside her, on the heat and the sense of power that emanated from him, that she hadn't been paying attention to the sounds around them. But once she did she heard just what Tyler had been talking about—a rhythmic croaking in the distance.

It made her think of beer commercials, and she laughed. "Not too melodic."

Tyler smiled his lopsided grin, putting that single dimple into his cheek. "Would you like music instead? I turned it off so we could talk, but I could turn it on again."

"No, this is nice." And she didn't want to lose his company for even a moment.

"I knew a girl once who had a thing for frogs," he said then.

"That sounds very kinky."

He laughed. "No, I mean she just collected frogs.

She had a couple of real ones, plus she had frog fig-urines and carvings and stuffed animals. She had frogs on her coffee mugs and on a T-shirt. She even had frog-print pajamas.''

"So you saw her in her pajamas," Willow said teas-ingly to hide the fact that it raised a hint of jealousy in her.

"Walked into that one, didn't I?"

"Why yes, you did."

"It'd be more incriminating if I'd seen her *without* the pajamas, though."

"True. It would have been worse if you'd said she had a frog tattoo somewhere not in plain sight."

But since the subject seemed to have been brought up, Willow seized the opportunity to pursue a question that had been niggling her.

"You said that first time we talked in my office that you'd probably met more than your fair share of women on the rodeo circuit. I've been wondering ever since if that meant you had rodeo groupies."

His dimple flashed again. "One or two," he an-swered, letting her know it was an understatement.

"So many that they're hard to remember, I'll bet." But she was hoping that wasn't really the case.

"There's too many people hanging around every rodeo to remember them all. Even without a concus-sion. But if you're askin' if I had my way with too many women to remember, the answer is not any-more."

Not as good an answer as no.

"Not anymore?" Willow repeated.

"At the start, Brick and I were pretty young, and having women throw themselves at us, well, it was every boy's dream. I have to admit we did some playin'."

"But only at the start?"

"Only until we wised up and realized we were tired of shallow relationships."

"So how many unshallow relationships have you had?"

"A couple."

"Two?"

"Two that were long-term."

"Did either of them get you close to marriage?" She already knew he'd never been married; he'd told her that in Tulsa.

"The first one broke up after four years because I wasn't ready to settle down."

"And the second one?"

"I was engaged to her, so that must mean I was close to getting married."

"What happened?"

"Every time we'd so much as talk about setting a date we'd go into weeks of arguments rather than actually doing it. We finally figured out that neither of us was sure enough we wanted to spend the rest of our lives together to get married at all. And once you figure that out *after* you've already gotten close it's hard to just go back to dating. We ended up going our separate ways."

"Do you think you'll ever want to get married? Or have a family?"

"Sure," he answered, easily enough to sound convincing and relieve some of the anxiety that had been unconsciously building in Willow. "Why do you think I bought such a big house? My folks were happy and in love with each other right to the end. I'd like that for myself."

Something was going through his mind, though, because suddenly his expression turned slightly serious, slightly ruminative, and he seemed to look more intently at her. But Willow couldn't tell what he was thinking.

Then he said, "I guess sometimes it's just hard to know who the right person might be."

"Oh, I don't know. I've seen two of my brothers find the right people in just the last few months, and when it happened they knew."

Tyler nodded, but Willow still had the impression something was confusing him.

But after a moment he let go of it and smiled at her in a softer, sexier way before he said, "I know I like being with you."

"Because I'm one of the guys?" she joked. It was something she'd heard too much in the past.

"One of the guys? Not hardly."

His porch light had come on automatically at dusk, and in its soft glow he held her eyes with his. And in them she saw that he meant what he said, that unlike all but one other man she'd ever known, he viewed her only as a woman and that it didn't cross his mind to consider her one of the boys.

Then he raised his fingertips to her cheek, caressing it as if he couldn't believe how smooth it was before he slid his hand to her chin to tilt it just so.

He closed the distance between them and pressed his mouth to hers in a kiss that was warm and soft and gentle. And only a prelude.

A prelude to a deeper kiss. To his arms coming around her and pulling her near enough to feel the hard wall of his chest. Near enough for her to wrap her arms around him as his lips parted and urged hers to part, too.

A small portion of her wondered at how easily she could be swept up in that kiss. But mostly she just let herself go. She let her lips open, and welcomed his tongue with her own. She let her hands fill themselves with the ebb and flow of the honed muscles of his back. She let her head fall back, indulged in the clean scent of his aftershave and let her engorged breasts nudge his pectorals as she felt her nipples harden through the sheer lace of her bra and the light fabric of her sundress. She let everything about him engulf her just the way it had that night in Tulsa, when nothing had mattered but this—being in his arms and feeling the way he made her feel.

But just then a sudden gust of wind swept in, bringing with it a cloud of dust to pummel them and interrupt what might have gone further than it should have.

Tyler ended the kiss abruptly, shielding her from

the barrage as best as he could. "Let's go in," he suggested in a voice deep with passion.

But Willow knew that wasn't wise. If they went in they would surely take up where they'd left off, and that might not be the best idea. Even if it was what she wanted all the way down to her toes.

"I should be going," she said instead. "It's getting late."

Tyler didn't argue, he just went on trying to shelter her from the wind whipping all around them as they stood and went to her truck.

He opened the door for her, and Willow got in in a hurry, before she lost her resolve.

But once she was safely behind the closed door and Tyler was leaning in through the open window she felt such a reluctance to go that she found herself inclined to tempt fate just to make sure she would see him again as soon as possible.

"I hope I won't be sorry for this. If you agree, I hope you won't be sorry for this, either. But we're having a barbecue tomorrow night. A family get-together, and everyone will be there—"

"Translation—all of your brothers?"

"Right. Even Jared is coming in from Texas for it. Anyway, if you're feeling brave, would you like to come as my guest?"

"Sure," Tyler said without a qualm.

"You don't want to think it over?"

He smiled. "I'm willing to wade through a few brothers to be with you."

"Good answer," she said, meaning it.

"What time shall I pick you up?"

"Six? It'll be at the family ranch. Actually, it's Bram's place."

"The sheriff."

"Right."

"Shall I wear a suit of armor?"

"Do you have one?"

He laughed again. "No, but I could see about renting one if you think I'll need it."

"Maybe they'll just play nice, since it'll be a family get-together and you'll be an invited guest. At least that's what I'm hoping."

"Me, too," Tyler said with yet another laugh. Then he aimed a warm, heart-meltingly devilish smile at her and said, "I'll see you at six."

He leaned in through the window and kissed her again, this time quickly, but with enough heat to light fires inside her.

And when he'd ended that one, it took Willow a moment to open her eyes and lower her chin in acceptance that that's all there was.

"Drive safe," he ordered her, straightening up and stepping away from her truck.

She could manage only a nod in response, so lost was she in trying to remember why she'd opted for going home, when what she wanted was to be back on that porch swing in his arms, being carried away by his kisses.

But she started the engine and put the truck in gear, waving as she drove off.

Into the twilight with the taste of Tyler still on her lips, the feel of his arms still around her.

And his baby within her to complicate it all unbelievably.

Chapter Seven

Tyler didn't ordinarily hang out at truck stops. But that was where he was the next afternoon. Sitting in his own truck, parked outside the dinerlike facade of the restaurant there.

For the first time since he'd moved to Black Arrow and been asking around, a conversation he'd had with a female clerk at the grocery store had garnered him the name of her roommate—a local woman who had been in Tulsa in mid-June.

Candy Wood.

She was a waitress at the truck stop just to the east of town, and, like the mystery woman, she apparently hadn't been to the rodeo. She'd been in Tulsa to collect her belongings after a breakup with a boyfriend.

Which, it seemed to Tyler, could also have led to a rash act like spending the night with a guy she'd met in a blues club.

So, armed with this information, Tyler had left the grocery store and gone directly to the truck stop, thinking the whole way, *This could be it....*

And yet, now that he was there, in close proximity to the person who might be the mystery woman, he didn't rush inside.

It wasn't as simple as he'd expected it to be.

Or maybe it wasn't as simple as it would have been a week ago. Before he'd met Willow.

His brother had thought he was crazy to make a major life decision based on what was little more than a hunch that if he settled in Black Arrow he'd come across the mystery woman again. Now that that might actually happen, and Tyler was reluctant to take the last few steps to potentially bring it about, Brick would think he was even crazier.

But he was definitely reluctant.

Because he wasn't sure what would happen if Candy Wood *was* the mystery woman.

Of course, what he was hoping would happen was that one sight of her would instantly bring back his memory—not only his memory of her and the night he'd spent with her, but of everything else he'd lost of that time frame shortly before the fall.

But what concerned him was what *else* might happen.

He'd felt driven to find the mystery woman, to

know what there was about her that had left him so distracted on that ride the next day that he'd ended up cutting short his whole career. He'd had the sense that there had been an instant bond between them. An attraction so strong, so powerful, it was unlike anything he'd ever experienced. Unlike anything he might ever find again. He'd had the sense that whatever had happened that night before the ride, with the mystery woman, was important enough to pursue.

But it was that very possibility that was tearing him up now. Because now there was Willow.

And while a few days earlier, when he'd thought that as much as he liked Willow, it would never be completely all right if he didn't find the mystery woman, now he wasn't so sure about that. He wasn't so sure Brick had been wrong when he'd said Tyler was putting too much weight on finding a woman he'd spent only one night with.

In fact, as Tyler sat there, watching other people go in and out of the restaurant, he wasn't so sure he even *wanted* to find the mystery woman. Not if it meant ruining things with Willow.

After all, wasn't there something to be said for a flesh and blood woman? A woman with luminous eyes and skin like satin and sugar-sweet lips?

There was. There was a lot to be said for it. A lot to be said for Willow. For a woman as nice as Willow. As fun and funny as Willow. As kind and considerate as Willow. As deep-down sexy as Willow.

Certainly there was a lot more to be said for her

than for a phantom woman who could easily be left in the mists of a memory too elusive to grasp.

"So let go of that other night and that other woman," he suggested to himself.

But even with his hand on the key, and with the intention of starting the engine and driving away, Tyler couldn't make himself do that, either.

If he didn't go into that truck stop and come face-to-face with the person who could be the mystery woman, he knew he'd be left wondering. Forever wondering if Candy Wood was the woman he'd moved to Black Arrow to find. Forever wondering if meeting her face-to-face would have brought back his memory.

No, he knew he had to go inside.

Whether he wanted to or not.

So, without much enthusiasm, Tyler pulled his keys from the ignition and finally got out of the truck.

The restaurant was bustling when he went in, and he was glad about that. It allowed him some anonymity as he glanced around the place, surreptitiously scanning the name tags each waitress wore until he located one that said Candy.

She was working the counter, and when a spot there opened up, Tyler took it.

She didn't come to wait on him immediately, so Tyler got the chance to get a good look at her before she saw him.

She was cute, but in a brassy sort of way. Her hair was aggressively blond and cut almost as short as a man's. Her eyes were big and brown, but shaded with too much blue shadow. She had full cheeks that were highlighted with slightly too much blush, and she wore lipstick as pink as bubble gum.

But she also had a nice smile and a body made for sin, and Tyler could see why so many of her customers were intent on flirting with her.

She approached him then, coffeepot in hand, and asked if he wanted a cup to start. He said he did, watching her all the while.

Her eyes were more on what she was doing than on him—or anyone else, for that matter—so it didn't strike him as strange that she didn't have any kind of instant recognition of him even if she was the mystery woman.

And Tyler was glad, because it gave him the opportunity to go on studying her, since no bells had gone off for him yet. In fact, she didn't seem familiar to him at all, and he didn't have a sudden return of any other memories, either.

She took his order, looking at the pad she wrote it on rather than him, and then left to jam the paper onto the wheel that hung from the top of the window opening into the kitchen.

Then she went on to tend to her other customers, and Tyler continued to study her.

He tried hard to see something he recognized in the angle of her head when she turned it a certain way. To figure out if her laugh was familiar when she responded to something another waitress said. He tried hard to know if he'd ever seen that walk before, or anything else about her, for that matter.

But there wasn't so much as a glimmer of memory, and by the time she brought him his club sandwich, he decided maybe he ought to engage her in conversation to get her to actually take a look at him in case she might recognize him.

"You wouldn't have been in Tulsa recently, would you?" he asked as if she did look familiar to him.

She finally glanced at his face. "As a matter of fact I was," she said curiously. "I was there in June."

"Me, too. Did you get to see the rodeo that was there then?" he asked, testing.

"I'm not into the cowboy thing."

"Ah. So what did you do there for fun?"

"Nothing much."

"You didn't even get one night out on the town? Say, at a blues club?" he prompted, even though it was becoming clear she didn't know him.

"I hate blues."

"And I don't look like anyone you might have met when you were there?" he persisted, just to be sure.

"I didn't meet anyone there. I was with friends. And no, you don't look like anyone I know," she said decisively.

Decisively enough to convince him.

So she wasn't the mystery woman.

Tyler nodded. "My mistake."

"That's okay. People are always thinkin' I'm somebody else," she said facetiously, as if it was a common pickup line.

Then she left him to his food and his thoughts.

It was strange, but if this had happened a week ago he probably would have come away from it feeling discouraged, dejected, and defeated.

But now he only felt relieved.

More than relieved, he actually felt good. Light-hearted and free. He felt as if he'd dodged a bullet.

So what was he doing, chasing shadows when he didn't really want to catch them? he asked himself.

Okay, so he'd based the biggest decision of his life on the idea that meeting the mystery woman had been his destiny, and that it was still part of that destiny to find her again, to be with her.

But what if that wasn't the case? What if Willow was his destiny instead? What if his whole hunch about coming to Black Arrow was really destiny leading him to her?

It was a surprisingly nice thought.

Except for one thing.

He'd also been convinced that finding the mystery woman would help him get his memory back. And if he stopped trying to find the mystery woman altogether, it also meant that he would be giving up the hope that the mystery woman would fill that gap for him.

And that wasn't something he was ready to do.

On the other hand, what if he stopped actively looking for the mystery woman? What if he really did leave it up to fate and let himself relax about it?

Hell, Brick and the doctors, too, had thought he'd be better off to do that from the start, to take the pressure off himself and just let things run their course. They'd thought he'd have a chance of regaining his memory by doing that alone.

So what if he gave in to that theory?

That felt okay, too. Maybe not quite as good as he'd felt when he'd realized Candy Wood wasn't the mystery woman, but pretty good all the same.

Because if he just left the future to fate, if he just let things run their course—including anything to do with the mystery woman—then he could also let things run their course with Willow.

And if fate or destiny put the mystery woman in his path again? He'd just see where things stood with Willow when it happened, and how he felt about her, how he might feel about the mystery woman. And he'd just play it by ear.

But in the meantime he wasn't going to put himself through any more of the kind of misery he'd felt coming to this truck stop, he decided. He wasn't going to do any more asking around about women who might have been in Tulsa in June.

He was going to hope his memory came back on its own, and trust in destiny to take care of the rest.

Candy Wood returned to ask if he wanted anything else, and left his check when he said he didn't.

And as Tyler paid the bill, he marveled all over

again at how relieved he was that she hadn't turned out to be the mystery woman.

And that was when it struck him that no matter who she turned out to be, if he ever actually did find the mystery woman she would have a very long way to go to compare with Willow.

At least in his eyes.

To say Willow was nervous about taking Tyler to her family barbecue was an understatement. She couldn't have been more nervous if she were about to undergo brain surgery.

And not only was she stressed about how her brothers might act with Tyler, about how they might treat him, she was also stressed about what to wear.

Normally she would have shown up at something like this in jeans and an oversize T-shirt—completely sexless tomboy clothes.

She didn't ever want Tyler to see her like that, but she knew that dressing in anything she *did* want him to see her in would only compound things with her brothers. And in the process, make it worse for Tyler. Not to mention opening the door to a rash of teasing remarks for herself, too.

It was all just so complicated, and there was a part of her that couldn't help regretting the impulse she'd acted on when she'd invited him to this gathering.

Of course, if she hadn't acted on that impulse she wouldn't have been able to see him today, and she wouldn't have liked that, either.

In any case, depending on what happened between herself and Tyler when it came out that she was pregnant, she wanted some sort of groundwork laid with her family. She wanted them to at least have met him.

But with only fifteen minutes before he picked her up, she didn't have time to worry, she just had to pick out something to wear and put it on.

Thoughts of Tyler and wanting to wow him prevailed, and she grabbed a pair of white Capri pants and a teal-blue, spandex tank top.

On went the slacks. Then on went the tank top, and she stopped short as she looked at herself in the full-length mirror.

Her breasts had gone up a cup size by the time she'd made it to the doctor to confirm her pregnancy. But almost overnight they seemed to have grown at least one size more. She was nearly voluptuous, and it amazed her.

She took a long look from the front, then turned to the side and stared at herself from that angle, thinking that she could wow just about anybody with those puppies.

It was great.

But it was the last thing she wanted her brothers to notice about her.

Still, she was so thrilled to have a fuller, more womanly body that she just couldn't make herself take off the tank top. After all, it wouldn't be long before her middle would be expanding at an even more rapid rate and ruin the effect.

But what she could do was cover up a little, she decided.

So she grabbed a white cotton blouse to wear over the tank top and her wonderful new bustline, leaving the blouse unbuttoned and untucked so there was only the slightest hint of what was underneath.

Then she hurried to apply blush and mascara—hoping her brothers wouldn't notice that, either—and brushed her hair, leaving it to hang loose and falling over her shoulders so that it, too, camouflaged her new profile.

The doorbell rang as she was putting on lipstick— also lightly—and the butterflies in her stomach took wing all over again.

"Please don't let this be a disaster," she said to no one in particular as she went to open the door.

Tyler was standing on the landing outside, and the minute he saw Willow, his handsome, clean-shaven face lit up with a smile that made any risk she was taking seem worth it.

He was dressed simply in cowboy boots, a pair of black jeans and a gray Henley T-shirt with the sleeves pushed up to his elbows. But he couldn't have looked any better in a tuxedo. The jeans were just tight enough to accentuate the thick-muscled thighs that had no doubt come from years of gripping the sides of bucking broncos, and the T-shirt hugged his broad shoulders, powerful pectorals and beautiful biceps like the caress Willow's hands were instantly itching to bestow.

"Sorry if I'm late," he was saying when Willow caught up from the time-delay of looking at him. "I ran some bushels of apples over to the general store on my way."

"That's okay, I wasn't ready myself," she said, pushing the screen open for him. "Come on in. I just have to grab the batch of brownies I made for dessert and we can go."

"You look great, by the way," he said to her back as she went to the counter to get the platter piled with decadent chocolate confections.

The compliment puffed out her chest even more as she spun around to face him again. "You, too," she said, meaning it.

Tyler held the screen open for her this time, pulling the main door closed behind them as they both stepped out onto the landing.

"Shall we walk or drive to this one?" he asked then.

"Drive. The ranch is about twenty minutes outside of town."

Tyler's truck was parked at the curb at the bottom of the steps, and he made sure to open that door for her, too, taking the dish of brownies from her while she got in, and returning them once she had.

She indulged in watching him when he rounded the front of the truck, appreciating the sight of his very straight back and that perfect derriere. That perfect derriere that she'd once seen bare...

But that was the last thing she wanted to be thinking

about. Especially since she could feel her nipples hardening in response, and that would never do.

She steadfastly continued to stare out the windshield as he got behind the wheel, willing her mind to keep to a more appropriate path and her nipples to calm down. Which wasn't easy, since they suddenly seemed so ultrasensitive she thought she could feel every fiber of the tank top against them.

"Where to?" Tyler asked after he'd started the engine and put the truck into gear.

Willow was grateful that he seemed completely unaware of the effect he was having on her, and gave him directions, still without so much as glancing at him.

Luckily, he was busy pulling away from the curb, and didn't seem to notice that, either.

"Is this barbecue for a special occasion?" he asked as he maneuvered the streets of Black Arrow.

"It's for my cousin Jesse. He's an agent with the National Security Agency in Washington, D.C."

"Really?"

"Really."

"That's interesting."

"He's an interesting guy. And since he's home for a visit right now we all wanted to get together to see him."

"So I'm up against four brothers *and* a cousin?"

"Five cousins. Although one of them is a girl, so she shouldn't give you any trouble. And my cousin Billy is out of the country."

"Eight guys are going to want to string me up for being with you?" Tyler said with a chuckle that still sounded undaunted.

If her brothers and her cousins all knew Tyler had gotten her pregnant, that might actually be the case. But since they didn't, she said, "My brothers can always count on my cousins' help if they want it, but usually—"

"They don't need it," he guessed.

Willow laughed. "Well, no, they don't usually need it. But what I was going to say was that my cousins don't have a thing about me actually seeing someone of the opposite sex. In fact, they've been known to give my brothers a hard time about always sticking their noses into my business."

"But it doesn't help?"

"My brothers just think they're looking out for their little sister, and no one ever manages to make them see it any differently."

They'd arrived at the ranch by then, and Tyler found a place to park in front of the patrol car.

"I guess this'll be interesting," he said, inclining his head in a kind of shrug. "Any words to the wise before we go in?"

"Don't touch me." Not an order she *wanted* to give, when having Tyler touch her was something she seemed to be craving more and more each time she saw him. "If you even take my hand for some reason or pat my arm they'll consider it pawing me and be all over you."

"Okay. No touching."

"And don't call me Will."

"Is that your request or is that a suggestion because of your brothers?"

"Both. They'll say you're trying to be one of us when you aren't one of us, and it'll tick them off."

"I wouldn't call you Will, anyway. Anything else?"

"Once a guy I went out to dinner with tried to feed me a bite of potato salad and ended up with a full plate of food in his lap."

"I won't try to feed you. Anything else?"

"That's all I can think of off the top of my head. Specifically, anyway."

"So I should just keep my distance."

"Not *too* much distance," she heard herself say before she realized she was going to.

It made Tyler smile a sexy smile that said he knew exactly what she was thinking. "Not *too* much distance. Got it," he said, as if confirming a command. Then he said, "Is it safe to go in now?"

"I don't know about safe, but I guess we probably should."

Tyler got out of the truck and came around to open her door, taking the brownies from her but not offering her a hand to help her down.

It was a silly thing, since Willow didn't need his help, but she felt a twinge of resentment toward her brothers for the omission that had surely come as a response to the no-touching rule.

Once she was out of the truck, Tyler closed the door but kept hold of the brownies.

"I can take those," Willow assured him.

But he pulled them out of her reach. "I might need them as weapons."

Willow laughed at his joke, but thought that he didn't know how right he might be.

She led the way into the house without knocking or even calling hello. The living room was empty, but they could hear voices coming from the rear, and that's where she headed.

Her aunt Alice was there with Jenna, Willow's cousin Sky, plus her new sister-in-law Kerry and Kerry's three-year-old daughter, Peggy, who was busy chasing an ice cube across the floor.

Willow introduced Tyler to her aunt, her cousin and Jenna, as well as to the woman her brother Jared had fallen in love with when Peggy had slipped into a drainage system he had been working on that summer. Jared had rescued the little girl, and he and Kerry had married soon after.

Tyler's greetings from the women of the family were open and friendly as Alice took the brownies from him and Jenna got him a beer. But then Bram came in from the backyard and stopped dead in his tracks the minute he saw him.

"I didn't know you were bringing someone, Willow," he said without taking his eyes off Tyler.

It was not a warm welcome. Especially when it was

accompanied by a scowl that would have been more fitting if Tyler had been holding them at gunpoint.

"I thought it would be a good way for Tyler to meet a lot of people at once," she explained.

"Hello again," Tyler interjected.

For a moment Bram just went on giving him a hard stare. Then, in a less than friendly tone, he said, "Tyler, isn't it?" as if he wasn't sure about the name.

"You know it is," Jenna said with a scolding edge in her voice.

Still without taking his eyes off Tyler, Bram called over his shoulder, "Ashe. Jared. Logan. You want to come in here a minute? There's someone who wants to meet you," he said facetiously.

"Bram..."

Both Willow and Jenna said it at the same time. But part warning, part impatient tones that harmonized together didn't faze the sheriff. He just went on pinning Tyler in place with cold eyes.

"It's okay," Tyler said, as if he wasn't at all concerned about holding his own. "I do want to meet your brothers."

Whether that was true or not, in came Willow's other three brothers, to stand like a wall with Bram and bore into Tyler with their eyes.

"Tyler, these are my brothers," Willow said with a sigh, pointing as she named them each in turn. "Guys, this is Tyler Chadwick. He just moved into the old Harris place."

"And he's our guest," Jenna added pointedly.

None of them said so much as a hello. But again Tyler ignored their intimidating rudeness and stepped forward to shake their hands.

Each of her brothers hesitated before accepting, letting him know through the process that they were really only pacifying the women who were looking on.

But even that didn't seem to disturb Tyler. He merely met their stares and waited them out, until each one of them shook his hand.

It was excruciating for Willow, and the moment all her brothers had complied, she stepped up and said, "Let's go out back so you can meet my great-grandfather and my uncle and the rest of my cousins."

"Okay," Tyler agreed. Then, to her brothers, he said, "Nice to meet you all," and stepped around them.

"Sorry about that," Willow said under her breath when they'd left them behind.

"It's pretty much what I expected. Except that I'm still in one piece. So don't worry about it."

Willow appreciated the levity he put into that, and had the urge to take his hand, to squeeze it in thanks. But of course she couldn't do that, and again felt a twinge of resentment for having to refrain.

There were picnic tables set up out back where a large barbecue was already red-hot and ready to go.

The rest of Willow's cousins were gathered not far from the barbecue, and since they were nearest to the back door, too, Willow led Tyler to them and performed those introductions first.

Unlike her brothers, Seth, Shane and Grey, and Jesse, the guest of honor, all offered Tyler a hand to shake and actually made congenial conversation before Willow urged him on to the picnic table where her uncle Thomas sat with George.

Both older men stayed seated when they approached, and Willow knew her uncle and her great-grandfather liked that Tyler called them each "sir" when she introduced him, and shook their hands, too.

They invited them to sit, and Willow's cousin Jesse joined them, too.

But they hadn't chatted for long when Bram came to stand at the end of the table and glare at Tyler.

"We need to talk about some private family business, so if you wouldn't mind, you could go over and keep an eye on those burgers on the barbecue."

"You can talk to me another time, Bram," Willow said through clenched teeth, before Tyler could respond.

But Tyler still took her brother in stride. "That's okay. I'm happy to help," he said amiably, getting up from the picnic bench.

"Then I'll help, too," she said defiantly.

But as she tried to get up, her big brother laid a hand on her shoulder and said, "This is important."

"Nothing's that important."

"This is."

"It's all right. I don't mind," Tyler assured her as he headed for the barbecue.

"When are you going to grow up?" Willow snapped at her brother out of frustration.

But Bram ignored the question and said, "I've filled Jesse in on what's going on around here with Gloria's letter and the deed. He's on his way back to D.C., so he's going to look into the trust fund and the property in Georgetown and report back."

"Good," Willow said to her cousin. "It should help for us to know what we're dealing with."

"I'm happy to help, too," Jesse said, repeating Tyler's words with an amused half smile.

Something suddenly seemed to tickle their great-grandfather, because his weathered face erupted in a knowing smile as he nodded his head sagely, as if he were belatedly approving of the plan.

Then he said to Jesse, "It's good you'll be looking for the answers. The raven who seeks will find the heart's truth."

Willow never knew quite what to say to those morsels of Comanche wisdom her great-grandfather spouted out of the blue.

But they were all spared the need to comment when her aunt Alice came out the back door and saw Tyler running the barbecue.

"Why is our guest doing the cooking?" she said loudly enough and in a sufficiently outraged tone that even Bram got to his feet in a hurry to take over.

"He looked like the best man for the job," Bram said, with an underlying derogatory note in his voice.

Alice was having none of that, though. She said,

VICTORIA PADE   169

"Mind your manners, Bram." Then she hooked her
arm through Tyler's and brought him back to Willow's
side. "Guests of the Coltons don't do the work around
here. They just enjoy our company," she proclaimed
as she deposited Tyler on the picnic bench once more.

The remainder of the evening was uneventful, but
not entirely pleasant. It was difficult to enjoy it when
only Logan—the more laid-back and jovial of her
brothers—made any friendly overtures to Tyler, while
the rest of her siblings watched him like hawks ready
to pounce on their prey. Her other relatives went out
of their way to be hospitable to blunt the effect, but it
still couldn't completely compensate, and as soon as
it was polite, Willow suggested she and Tyler say
good-night and leave.

"I'm sorry for that," she apologized for the second
time as Tyler opened the truck door for her. "Every
time I bring someone around them I hope they'll have
stopped the big brother routine. And tonight, since
Bram and Jared are happily in love, I'd hoped that
might lighten them up. But apparently not."

"It's okay," Tyler said, as if it really was. Then he
got behind the wheel, started the engine and drove
away from the ranch.

The farther they got from it the more the tension of
the evening seemed to ease. By the time they reached
the Feed and Grain, Willow had relaxed enough to
realize she wasn't ready for her time with Tyler to
come to an end yet. In fact, it was as if it hadn't really
begun.

So, when Tyler parked at the curb, she said, "Let me buy you a glass of lemonade to make up for this."

"Deal," he agreed without hesitation, making her feel instantly better about almost everything.

Willow had left all the windows in her apartment open to catch the cooling night air, so it was pleasant when they went inside. Unfortunately, or she might have had an excuse to take off her overblouse the way she was dying to.

But as it was, she merely poured two glasses of lemonade and they took them into the living room.

They sat together on the sofa as if it were a long-standing tradition. Both of them in the center. Not too close, but close enough so that Willow could smell the lingering scent of his aftershave.

"So you said *every* time you bring someone around your brothers you hope it will be better. How many *every times* have there been?" Tyler asked once they were settled and had tasted the lemonade.

"Three," Willow answered, without having to calculate.

"Come on," he said dubiously. "Only three?"

"Exactly three."

"How can that be?"

"Pretty easily. Especially when the first guy who kissed me ended up not living it down for a week."

"How did they manage that?" Tyler sounded amused and curious, but not disapproving in spite of the evening her brothers had just put him through.

"They caught us kissing behind the school—"

"Your first kiss?"

"My very first kiss."

"And you were how old?"

"Fourteen. And to tell you the truth, I found out later that Herbie only kissed me on a dare even then. I was just too much of a tomboy for any guy to really be interested."

"If this Herbie was only kissing you on a dare he deserved whatever your brothers dished out. Which was what?"

"Jared and Logan saw us and yanked Herbie away by the back of his shirt. Herbie landed on his rear end— embarrassed more than anything—and Jared and Logan just did the standard stay-away-from-our-sister tirade and let him go. But the next day in the locker room they got hold of Herbie and covered him from head to toe in drawings of lips. Drawings they made with permanent red ink markers. It took about a week for it to all wear off, and in the meantime Herbie had to walk around like that, the laughingstock of the school. It was like making him an advertisement for what would happen to any guy who came near me."

"Okay," Tyler said, laughing at the anecdote. "That was number one. What about number two?"

"Billy Shultz. I was seventeen. And he was new in town."

"So he hadn't been warned off by the Herbie incident."

"Right. There was a reverse dance in December of my junior year of high school—that's where the girls asked the guys. I knew no one else would go with me and I kind of liked Billy, so I thought I'd give it a try.''

"And get your second kiss?"

"Oh, no, it never got that far. Billy was holding my hand when we went into the diner for dinner before. Bram and Jared were there and saw us. They joined us—uninvited, and even after my every attempt to discourage them. They made sure Billy knew to keep his hands to himself, and wouldn't leave us alone until Billy swore he would. Then they moved to the table next to ours."

"So good old Billy could still be under their scrutiny."

"Exactly. We tried to ignore them, but as we were eating, Billy offered me a bite of his potato salad."

"And you took it."

"It was just a bite of potato salad. It couldn't have been more innocent," Willow assured him.

"But Billy ended up with his food in his lap."

"And I never got to the dance at all."

"Or asked out by Billy Shultz again, either, I imagine."

"Definitely not."

"Which brings us to number three."

That one was a little more painful, and it must have shown in her expression because before she'd said anything, Tyler put his nearly empty lemonade glass on the coffee table and took her hand, smoothing the back with tiny circles of his thumb.

"Number three wasn't just kid stuff, was it?" he asked compassionately.

"No, it wasn't. I was really...involved with Shawn."

"'Involved' meaning in love?"

Willow nodded her head as she set her glass on the table, too, making sure not to pull her hand from the warmth of his because it felt so good to have it enveloped in that big, strong grasp.

"I met Shawn at the start of my senior year in college," she explained. "I was away from home, and even though I was still more tomboy than femme fatale, Shawn seemed to see past that and asked me out anyway."

"Good for Shawn."

"And good for me. We dated all year and we were getting pretty serious so I thought I should bring him home over spring break to meet everyone. By then I thought we'd all grown up enough that my brothers might just accept him."

"No such luck," Tyler guessed.

"No such luck," she confirmed. "That time they called it trial by fire."

"That doesn't sound good."

"Especially not for Shawn. My brothers said they just wanted to make sure he was man enough for me. I told Shawn he didn't have to prove anything, but he wouldn't listen. He was sure he could outsmart them— he was more brain than brawn, and I guess in a way he thought he was better than my brothers."

"It'd be tough enough just being equal."

"Exactly. And Shawn was...well, Shawn was good with books, but my brothers didn't pass out a manual."

"What was the trial by fire?"

"They took him camping. Without any supplies."

"So he had to look for wood to make a fire—"

"Without matches," Willow explained.

"And he had to hunt or fish or forage for food."

"With bows and arrows."

"And he had to sleep under the stars."

"With only a single blanket, not even a sleeping bag. And they deserted him. Well, they didn't really. They were keeping an eye on him, but kept out of sight, so poor Shawn thought he was on his own."

Tyler grimaced. "Scared the guy pretty good, I'll bet."

"*Terrified* was the word Shawn used when they got him home the next day."

"And instead of swearing never to fall for another of your brothers' pranks, he dumped you?"

"He actually seemed to sort of blame me. I'd warned him not to go along with anything they wanted him to do, but somehow Shawn felt like I'd set him up. He said he didn't want anything to do with someone who would bring him into a situation like that."

"So much for outsmarting your brothers, too. But apparently good old Shawn wasn't taking any of the responsibility, huh?"

"No, he wasn't."

"But you really liked the guy and you were still sorry to have it end with him," Tyler concluded. "And there hasn't been anyone since then?"

"I came back to Black Arrow after I graduated. Back to where I'm the tomboy little sister of four brothers who are known to be tough on any man who looks at me twice."

Tyler looked at her then, top to bottom to top again, with a split second pause when he came across her breasts both times. "Tomboy?" he repeated.

"Hard to change the image people have of you," she said, as if that outward image hadn't only recently been altered to intrigue him.

"Tomboy isn't what I see," he said, his voice suddenly lower, more intimate.

"What do you see?" she asked, flirting but also dying to know.

"I see a beautiful woman who mixes strength with softness, self-sufficiency with a tender heart, independence with consideration, brains and ability with sexiness that's just under the surface waiting to be let out. In short, you can hold your own in a man's world *and* among women."

Willow liked that description a whole lot better than *tomboy.*

She also liked the way Tyler was still looking at her, with so much heat in his green eyes she could actually feel herself warming.

He was still holding her hand, only now he reached his free hand to tilt her chin so he could press his mouth to hers in a kiss that suddenly made the whole miserable night worth it. A kiss that instantly tightened her nipples and made her aware all over again of her new and improved breasts.

Tyler's lips parted over hers and his tongue didn't hesitate to pay a call, urging her to play, to dance, to match him game for game.

And that's just what Willow did, losing herself in his kiss, in the wonderful spring-rain scent of him, in the warmth of his body all around her and the tingles of excitement he was setting off in his slow, sexy massage of her hand.

Those newly engorged breasts had a mind of their own and were craving at least the pressure of his chest against them. So much so that Willow reached her free arm around him, not quite pulling Tyler to her the way she wanted, but at least giving herself the opportunity to get a little nearer to him.

Tyler took the cue—or maybe it was just what he wanted, too, because he wrapped his arms around her and did what she hadn't had the courage to do. He closed the space between their bodies by bringing her up against him so that her full breasts nudged his hard pectorals, setting off sparks of delight in Willow.

Every minute of the night she'd spent with him in Tulsa was vivid in her mind, and as good as it had felt, nothing had felt as good as the meeting of her breasts with his chest did now. It was as if her body had been only half-awake before and now was fully alive and aware of every tiny nuance.

And yearning for more than tiny nuances.

Yearning so much that she grew brave enough to pull Tyler's shirt from his waistband so she could slip her own hands underneath to press her palms against his back.

An expanse so incredible it helped distract her as she relearned the satin-over-steel textures, as she rode the rise and fall of muscles and tendons, as she indulged in the hot sweetness of his bare skin.

He abandoned her mouth then, placing teasing kisses on her jawbone, down the side of her neck, even on her shoulder when he'd eased off her blouse.

The blouse fell naturally, finally freeing her the way she'd wanted to be free all evening, with only the tight tank top separating them.

Then Tyler reclaimed her mouth with his in an even more sensual, open kiss that she answered only too willingly as his hands traveled from her back to her shoulders and down her arms, pulling her even closer.

Willow ached for more, for him to touch more than her arms, and her body sent that message all on its own by arching back before she even realized she was going to.

That was when Tyler moved a hand to the side of her breast, hesitating, as if to give her the chance to stop him before he actually took the entire orb into his palm.

But stopping him was not on Willow's mind. In fact, every inch of her was crying out for him not to be so cautious, so considerate, to get on with it before she went out of her mind with craving his touch.

Then he did get on with it. His hand eased forward, finally engulfing one of those oh-so-sensitive orbs.

Willow couldn't help the moan that rumbled from her throat. She couldn't help the even greater arch of her spine. She couldn't help digging her fingers slightly into his back as a pleasure sharp enough to make her gasp rippled through her.

He didn't waste much more time before he found his way underneath the tank top, and that only increased everything tenfold, making her writhe slightly as that powerful palm closed over her knotted nipple. As he kneaded her breast. As he teased it with fingers that explored her flesh, that traced around that hardened crest, that gently pinched and tugged and teased her until other parts of her body began to come to life, too. Parts much lower and much more secret. Parts that suddenly screamed for the attention of those wonderfully adept hands. Parts that screamed for more than that, for that glorious portion of him that had taken her to heights she'd never even known existed only months before.

But something about that intense desire for him to fill the aching need between her legs reminded her of the consequences of that other time when she'd lost control so completely with him. It reminded her that she had set a goal for herself, a goal of letting him get to know the real Willow.

And the real Willow wouldn't have gone even as far as she already had, let alone any further.

"We should stop," she breathed when reason prevailed and she managed to tear herself from his kiss.

Her request lacked conviction, but it was all Tyler needed to hear to slide his hand out from under her top and do exactly as she'd asked.

"Was I out of line?" he asked in a voice raspy enough to let her know he'd been wanting more, too.

"No," she said through the haze of desire that was still coursing through her and labeling her a traitor to her own body. Then, in a firmer, more convincing tone, she added, "No! It's just that I don't want to move too fast." This time, anyway, even though it was a little late for that policy to be put into effect.

"You're probably right," he said, agreeing without sounding convinced.

He stood then, taking a breath so deep she saw the rise and fall of his chest as he did. Then he held out his hand and said, "Come on, walk me to the door."

Willow complied, grateful that he was taking her abrupt ending so amiably. And grateful, too, that he kept hold of her hand the whole way through the kitchen.

"I understand your first order from the Feed and Grain will be ready for delivery tomorrow," she said as they reached the door, just to make conversation and buy herself a few more precious moments with him.

"Do you do the deliveries in person?" he asked

with a mischievous smile and a voice full of insinuation.

"Not since I was seventeen."

"You don't even go along to supervise now and then?"

"Well, there are always exceptions," she lied.

"You could come out to supervise and I could bring you back into town later, say, for dinner and maybe ice cream afterward."

"Oh, well, if there'll be ice cream…" she joked, as if that were the selling point when, in fact, the only selling point she needed was Tyler himself.

"So you'll come?"

"You'll have to be the last delivery of the day," she warned.

"I'm fine with that," he assured her, looking deep into her eyes.

"Then I guess I'll be there," Willow said, her voice suddenly soft and breathy.

Tyler kissed her again then, a tender kiss that was still so sexy it made her sparkle inside. But he left it at that one last kiss, squeezed her hand and then let himself out and closed the screen between them before he said, "Good night."

"See you tomorrow."

He only nodded in response, but she thought he took a last glance at her chest while he was at it.

It delighted her no end to think of sending him away longing for her, and she couldn't suppress the smile on her face as she watched him go down the stairs.

But when she found herself in bed shortly afterward the tables were turned.

Because as she lay there in the dark, she remembered all too well what it had felt like to have his hands on her bare, ultrasensitive breasts.

And she discovered that she had a potent longing of her own to wrestle with.

A longing for Tyler to be lying there with her.

Kissing her again.

Touching her again.

Making love to her again.

Just the way he had in Tulsa...

Chapter Eight

Mondays were always hectic at the store, and to make matters worse, Carl was grumpy. It was Willow's fault. First thing in the morning she'd asked him if he would do the delivery to Tyler after closing. Carl was not happy to make any delivery himself, and he certainly wasn't thrilled to do one that late in the day. But Willow couldn't get away before closing time, and she didn't want to entrust the delivery truck to their high school driver overnight. So that left Carl, who agreed to do it, but not without grumbling.

Any other time Willow would have lost patience with it. But as it was, she was too glad that Tyler wanted to see her to care, so she just endured the grumbling.

When Carl began to load the truck at six she went upstairs to change. She was in a hurry, but still managed a quick shower before she put on the outfit she'd decided on earlier, when she'd been struggling to get down a piece of dry toast to help the morning sickness.

She didn't want to look as if she'd done anything but come from work, so she opted for her favorite blue jeans and the new white wrap shirt that was held together by one simple tie at the right side of her waist. She thought the blouse softened and feminized the blue jeans, but still didn't make it seem as if she'd taken any special pains just to make a feed delivery.

She did put on blush and mascara, though, and she twisted her hair into a roll at her crown, held there with the chopsticks, while spiky ends stuck out every which way.

When she judged herself presentable, she slipped her feet into a pair of sandals and rushed out of her bedroom.

But she got only as far as the living room before she stopped short.

Bram was sitting on her sofa.

"I didn't know you were here," she said, startled.

Bram had his feet on her coffee table, his arms stretched along the top of the back cushion, and the expression on his face was no happier than Carl's had been through the last eight hours.

"Carl said you were up here getting ready to deliver feed with him," Bram said, as if he were accusing her of a crime.

Willow had expected at least one of her brothers to show up today to grill her over Tyler and his presence at the barbecue the previous evening. When that hadn't happened she'd hoped they might have just accepted it and opted to leave her alone about it.

She should have known better.

"Carl must be about loaded up by now," she said, hinting that she didn't want this to take long.

But Bram ignored the hint. He just stared at her and said, "So are you dating this Chadwick guy?"

Willow felt the tension build in her, but she tried to tamp it down. She also made a quick decision not to deny too much. After all, she'd wanted the ice broken between her brothers and Tyler, she'd wanted to lay some groundwork, and to pretend she and Tyler were merely friends now would not aid that cause.

With that in mind, she said, "I've seen him a couple of times and I'm getting to know him a little." Okay, so that wasn't an outright admission that they were *dating,* but it was still something.

It just didn't fool her brother.

"Sounds like dating to me."

So much for soft-pedaling.

Still, Willow returned Bram's stare without backing down.

"You like this guy?" her brother asked, as if he couldn't believe it.

Again Willow held her ground. "He's nice. He's interesting. He's fun to be with. He's—"

"You like him."

"There's nothing wrong with that, Bram."

"Depends."

"On what?"

"On a lot of things," her brother said vaguely. But apparently he didn't want to expound on it, because then he said, "Carl says that he has to work late just so he can deliver you to this guy along with the feed order."

Maybe she shouldn't have had so much patience with Carl's attitude.

"Carl doesn't have any business complaining to you. I *asked* him to do this, I didn't order him to, and he agreed. Plus I'm paying him double time."

"To deliver you to Chadwick."

"To deliver Tyler's order to him. We've made after-hours deliveries before. It just so happens that I'm going along because I have dinner plans with Tyler and this kills two birds with one stone. It's no big deal."

"I don't know about this, Will," her brother said with a solemn shake of his head. And then, as if he just couldn't resist telling her what was wrong with liking Tyler, after all, he said, "The guy just moved to town. We don't know him or anything about him. He could have wives and kids in six other states."

"He doesn't."

"How can you be sure? Because he told you he doesn't?"

"He doesn't."

"We just don't want to see you get in over your head with somebody and get hurt."

Too late for the getting-in-over-her-head part. Maybe for the getting-hurt part, too, if things didn't pan out.

But she didn't say that.

She said, "*We* being you and Ashe and Logan and Jared."

"Who else?"

Willow took a deep breath, then sighed, making an effort to hold on to her temper. "Look, I know you guys mean well. I know you care about me and you think you need to look out for me and protect me, but I'm going to say this one more time—I'm a big girl, Bram. I can take care of myself. You and Ashe and Jared and Logan have to stop. If I need your help, I'll let you know. I'll scream it from the rooftop. But unless I do that, please, please, please stop this big brother routine you guys have always done. Especially with other guys. Or I'm liable to end up your poor, lonely, pitiful spinster sister who comes to holiday dinners wearing Fruit Loop jewelry."

That made him smile in spite of himself. "Fruit Loop jewelry?"

"That part got through to you, but you don't care about the poor, lonely, pitiful spinster part?"

"Of course I care about it. But that's not going to be you."

"How isn't it going to be me if you and Jared and Ashe and Logan scare off any guy who looks twice at me the way you've always done? I'm not a kid anymore, Bram. I'm a full-grown woman and I brought a perfectly nice man to a barbecue yesterday and my brothers treated him like he had a contagious disease he was about to infect me with. You have someone—you have Jenna. Jared has Kerry. Before long Ashe and Logan will have women in their lives. But what will I have if my brothers keep standing as a barrier between me and anyone of the opposite sex?''

Bram's expression had wrinkled up into a frown again, this one darker than the last one. "Have you been talking to Jenna about this?''

"Why? Because she said the same thing? No, I haven't been talking to Jenna about this. I don't have to talk to anyone about this to feel the way I do. I love you guys, but sometimes…sometimes you smother me.''

For a long moment Bram stared at her with that familiar scowl, and she wasn't too sure she hadn't said too much. That she hadn't hurt his feelings or made him mad.

But then he took a deep breath of his own and exhaled slowly. "So you want me—us—to butt out, is that it?''

"Butt out and be nice to people of the male persuasion who I might happen to bring around or be with when you meet me on the street. Is that asking so much?''

"Yes," he said frankly. But then he added, "I guess we could try, though. A little. Except if we see you doing something we know is stupid. Then we'll have to butt in.''

Too late for that, too. She'd already done the most stupid thing she could have done.

But she didn't say that, either.

Instead she said, ''All I'm asking at the moment is that you be polite and friendly to Tyler. I'm not doing anything stupid with him right now, I'm just getting to know him and letting him get to know me. No big deal.''

Bram didn't look convinced.

But he did finally pull his feet off the coffee table and stand.

''You're a big deal to us,'' he said seriously.

''Well, I don't want to be.''

''And we're never going to stop looking out for you. But maybe we could back off some. Give you a little space with this guy, if that's what you really want.''

''That's what I really want.''

''But we'll still be watching.''

Willow rolled her eyes and tried to be happy for even a small victory. ''Of course you will be.''

Tyler was waiting for Willow and the delivery when they arrived at his ranch. He was dressed in work clothes that he'd obviously been in since morning, because his jeans and his chambray shirt were soiled, and his face was shadowed with a full day's growth of beard.

The fact that he looked good to her in spite of it all let Willow know she was in trouble with this man. Well, more trouble than being pregnant by him.

But she tried not to think about the fact that even with him sweaty and dust-covered and bewhiskered, she could still have jumped his bones without a qualm.

Don't move too fast, she told herself, recalling her own comment to him the night before, when she'd stopped him before they'd actually made love.

She knew it was good advice and that she needed to follow it. But one look at him was enough to do her in, and watching him hoist feed sacks out of the back of the truck alongside Carl, watching his impressive muscles tensing under the weight, watching his tight derriere as he bent over to pile the sacks inside the big red barn was enough to weaken her knees and her will at once.

"She used to help with this," Carl pointed out crankily as they worked, hinting for her to lend a hand the way she would have several months earlier.

But Tyler said, "I wouldn't let her even if she wanted to," and that just left Carl to more grumbling.

Grumbling that continued right up until they were finished and Carl got back behind the wheel to drive off without so much as a goodbye to either of them.

But if Tyler noticed, he didn't seem to care. He removed his work gloves and then his cowboy hat, wiping dampness from his brow with the back of his arm and settling his gaze on Willow as if for the first time.

"Hi," he said in a tone that held an intimacy she was beginning to believe he reserved for her alone.

"Hi," she answered the same way.

"Sorry about this," he apologized, nodding down at himself to let her know he was referring to the way he looked. "I didn't want to clean up and then get all dusty from the feed sacks again so I figured I'd have to wait to shower. Do you mind?"

"No," she answered, not telling him she actually liked him all rugged and rustic and masculine.

"I promise I won't take long. And I made you fresh squeezed lemonade for the wait."

"Sounds good."

Tyler motioned toward the house, and that was where they headed. He held the back door open for her when they reached it, following her up the three steps into the mud room, where he hung his hat on a hook just inside the door. Then he washed his hands in the laundry basin and they went into the kitchen.

He filled two glasses with ice and lemonade from a pitcher in the refrigerator, handing her one and then nearly guzzling his before he said, "Make yourself at home. Turn on the television or the radio if you want. Or sit on the porch swing—it's shaded at this time of day and usually catches a breeze. Or whatever you feel like doing. I'll be back before you can miss me."

She doubted that, but she said, "Don't rush. I'll be fine."

She watched him go, and wondered at herself for thinking he even looked great with hat-hair.

But then he was gone and she was left to her own devices.

Sitting on the porch swing had been the most appealing of his suggestions, so Willow headed for the front of the house.

But halfway through the living room the fireplace mantel caught her eye. Unlike when she'd been there previously, it was no longer bare, but was now lined with framed photographs. She made a detour to be nosy.

There were pictures of a couple on their wedding day, and from the dated look of it and the resemblance between Tyler and both the bride and the groom, Willow had no doubt it was a portrait of his parents.

There were a few other family photographs of vacations and horseplay, of graduations and other school events. One snapshot was obviously taken at Christmas, of Tyler and his brother in footed pajamas.

There were also pictures that chronicled Tyler's and his brother's careers in rodeo.

It was easy to tell Brick was Tyler's brother because they looked so much alike, too. But Willow thought Tyler was the more handsome. There were shots of them riding bucking broncos and roping calves. There were photos of them celebrating victories with a wave of a hat in the air, with grins from ear to ear, with belt buckles held as trophies.

Tyler had loved what he'd done for a living before coming to Black Arrow. Before meeting her in Tulsa and taking that last ride. If he hadn't already told her that she would only have had to look at those photographs to know.

And yet he seemed to have accepted the ending of it all with aplomb. With grace and good humor.

She thought that said a lot about him. About the kind of man he was. A lot that she liked.

And she wondered whether, if and when she told him about the baby she was carrying, he would react the same way. If, once the shock had passed, he would accept it and adapt. Embrace it the way he appeared to have embraced his new life here.

She hoped so.

But that was really all she could do—hope. Because while somewhere in his thinking he had to have always known his rodeo days would come to an end, he wasn't likely to have planned for a woman he didn't even remember having met announcing she was pregnant with his child.

And there was no way to gauge how anyone would react to that.

Fear caused Willow to press a protective hand to her stomach, as if to shield her unborn baby from any negative response. And she couldn't help wondering if she would ever find the courage to actually tell Tyler at all.

"Hey, are you okay?"

Willow hadn't heard Tyler come down the stairs and the sound of his voice startled her.

"Great, now I've scared you, too. I'm sorry," he added, coming into the living room.

"It's okay." She quickly pulled her hand from her middle and put it in her pocket.

"Did my lemonade make you sick?"

"No, why?"

"You were holding your stomach."

"I'm fine. I was just snooping and you caught me at it," she said, as if that explained the hand pressed to her middle.

"It's not snooping to look at pictures that are out on display."

"They're nice," she said, to change the subject.

"Thanks."

"But you look so happy in the rodeo ones I'm surprised you've adjusted so well to not being able to do it anymore."

"Who says I'm well adjusted?" he joked.

"You're not pouting."

He laughed. "I'd get my rear end kicked if I was. Brick would never let me get away with that."

"And you're always in a good mood."

"Maybe it's the company I'm keepin'," he answered with a half smile that dimpled his cheek.

She wanted to accept the compliment, but her pleasure in it was dampened when she began to wonder one more thing. She began to wonder for the first time if being with her would help his attitude so much if he knew the truth about her. If he knew that they'd met before, spent the night together, and she was leaving him in the dark about it, leaving his memory blank when she could fill it in.

She was afraid he wouldn't be.

And worse yet, she was afraid that now, since she'd kept the truth from him, he might resent it when he realized it. When he realized that those good feelings she was helping him to have, those feelings she thought she might be arousing in him, were caused by someone who was essentially lying to him. Lying to him through omission if nothing else.

"Are you sure you're feeling okay? You don't have a drop of color in your cheeks. Maybe you should sit down," he stated, taking a closer look at her.

"I think I just need food," she said with forced brightness.

But apparently he bought it, because he just said, "Then we'd better get you some."

Tyler took her glass and set it on a nearby table before he ushered her out the front door to his waiting truck.

But after he'd handed her up into the passenger side, closed the door and was headed around the front end, Willow had trouble shaking the anxious, foreboding sense she had.

Because the bottom line was that she'd deceived him the night they'd met, and she was deceiving him again now.

Which was hardly a good basis on which to begin a relationship.

And even noticing how wonderful Tyler looked all cleaned up and dressed in jeans and a pale-blue Western shirt didn't help chase away her concerns about the course she'd embarked on with him.

And the very real possibility that it might all blow up in her face.

Dinner did nothing to calm Willow's nerves.

Tyler took her to a local steak house that was packed to the brim, and no sooner had they walked in the door than she heard her name called.

She scanned the crowded restaurant and finally caught sight of who it was trying to get her attention.

And of all the people in Black Arrow who it could have been, she was not happy to find it was her brother Bram.

He and Jenna were sitting in the center of the place, and Willow and Tyler had no choice but to go over and say hello.

Which was when Bram invited them to join him and Jenna rather than waiting for another table to open up.

Willow and Tyler didn't have much choice, so they took the two empty seats at the table and began what was essentially a grilling of Tyler by Bram.

It left Willow wishing her brother would have done more of what he'd done the previous evening, when all of her brothers had spent more time glaring at Tyler than talking to him. As it was, the meal couldn't end soon enough for her.

"I think the ice cream is going to have to be my treat to make up for that," she said when they finally got away from Bram the Interrogator and were back in Tyler's truck, headed away from the restaurant. "I didn't know my brother would be there tonight. I saw him just before I came to your place, but he didn't say anything about going out for dinner."

"It's okay," Tyler assured her, still in good humor and not nearly as ruffled as Willow was. "And the ice cream idea was mine, so I'm still buying. But what do you say we just get a pint to go and hide out at your apartment to eat it?"

"So we don't risk running into any more of my brothers and having to spend the rest of our evening with them? Good idea."

Tyler didn't confirm or deny her assumption, he just drove to the local ice cream parlor, where they decided on chocolate mousse ice cream with swirls of peanut butter through it, and counted themselves lucky to have run into only three people Willow knew, none of them her brothers.

· The ice cream was melting badly when they finally reached the Feed and Grain again, and since church choir practice had left no parking spots nearby, Tyler let Willow off right at the foot of the steps to her apartment, while he went in search of an opening farther away.

Willow was just glad to be back without any further encounters with her brothers, and climbed the stairs in a hurry to get her cold confection to the freezer.

She fumbled with her keys, keeping the dripping container away from her as she did.

Then she stepped into her kitchen.

It was dark by then and she reached for the light switch.

But before she could flip it on, a beefy arm came around her neck from behind, clamping back on her windpipe and yanking her up against an unyielding body.

The ice cream container hit the floor as she grasped the arm at her throat with both hands. But the man was stronger than she was, and even clawing at his arm to pull it away didn't faze him.

"Just give me the documents and you won't get hurt."

His hot breath smelled of onions and cigarettes, and her stomach lurched.

Willow didn't understand. Not what was going on. Not what he was saying. Nothing. She only struggled to breathe while her own pulse pounded like a jungle drum in her ears.

"I don't know—" she barely managed to gasp.

"The inheritance. I heard you found the papers for it. I want them. Now."

His voice was low and threatening. His arm was still tight across her throat. And Willow's legs felt as if they might buckle at any moment.

"—don't have them—"

The arm pressed harder, squeezing off her airway even more. "Don't be stupid. Just tell me where they are."

Tiny flickers of light flashed before her eyes and she thought she was going to pass out.

"—locked away...bank—"

There was pressure in her head. Ringing in her ears. Pain behind her eyes.

"Please..." she said as strongly as she could. "I can't breathe."

Then all at once something exploded behind her with a jolt that knocked her forward, free of the vice-like arm.

Willow gasped for breath, belatedly realizing that the man hadn't just released her, that there was more going on.

She turned and found Tyler pinning the man to her kitchen floor, one knee in the middle of his back, one hand wrenching up on the arm that had been around her neck, his other hand pressing the man's face into her linoleum.

"Are you all right?" Tyler demanded of her, his tone intense.

"I think so," she said in a feeble, raspy voice.

"Then get your brother over here before I make this guy sorry he was ever born."

The man was Kenny Randolph. Willow recognized him from the night she'd seen Bram talking to him after the carnival.

Once she'd called her brother, Tyler insisted she wait for Bram outside, where she was safe, while he kept Randolph restrained in her kitchen.

Bram and two of his deputies arrived fifteen minutes after her call. As the deputies went up to her apartment, Bram stayed with Willow, making sure she was all right and then asking what had happened.

Willow kept her arms wrapped around herself the whole time she gave her statement. It was the only way she could keep her hands from shaking, and she didn't want her brother to see that they were.

Then the deputies brought Randolph out, followed close behind by Tyler, and as Bram helped to put Randolph in one of the patrol cars, Tyler joined Willow.

Without a word he enveloped her in his strong arms and pressed her head to his chest, apparently not caring what his actions might set off in her brother.

And at that moment Willow didn't care, either.

She just let herself drink in the comfort of Tyler's big, solid body, because that hug was exactly what she needed.

"Are you okay?" he asked quietly, his breath a tiny gust in her hair.

"Thanks to you."

"I came upstairs and couldn't figure out why you hadn't turned on a light. Then, just as I got to the screen door, I saw you. You and that son of a...that guy."

"It's a good thing we didn't go in together," she said, her cheek still pressed to his pectorals.

"Your place is pretty torn up. He must have been ransacking it for a while before we got there," Tyler said, as if to warn her before she saw the place lighted.

"He was looking for something—documents I found the other day, which my grandmother left.

We've inherited a trust fund and some sort of property in Washington, D.C., and he wanted the papers to prove it. He wanted me to hand them over to him. But I didn't have them to give him. Bram took them to put in the safe at the bank.''

''Word leaked that you'd found the deed, but not that the papers were out of your hands, which was just what I was afraid of.''

It was Bram's voice filling in that detail. He was close enough to have heard them talking, even though Willow hadn't known her brother had rejoined them.

She didn't want to leave Tyler's arms, but she raised her head from his chest anyway and moved away from him.

And when she did she found her brother with a dark scowl on his face, whether because of the events of the evening or because of Tyler, she couldn't be sure.

''That's why I wanted you to come to my place to stay,'' Bram added.

''At least you have him in custody now,'' Willow reasoned. ''Maybe you'll be able to get to the bottom of everything else.''

Bram still didn't look happy.

But even so he angled his gaze toward Tyler and said, ''Thanks for doing what you did.''

Tyler waved it off as if he hadn't done anything. ''I'm just glad I was here.''

It didn't seem as if Bram wanted to go quite that far. Instead he looked at Willow again and said,

"You'd better come home with me. Your place is a wreck."

Willow shook her head, thinking as she had when her brother had wanted her to stay with him before that her morning sickness would be a dead giveaway if she did. "The real danger is over. I'll be fine here. But how did Randolph get in?"

"Through the back door to the store. Looks like he jimmied open the lock with a crowbar. One of my men boarded it up. We'll have to get it fixed in the morning. But that's another reason not to stay here tonight."

Willow still wouldn't agree, and with Kenny Randolph and both deputies waiting for him, Bram couldn't argue for long. He finally had to concede.

"I'll send a patrol car by here every twenty minutes all night long," he said then. "But if you get nervous, just call and I'll come get you."

"I will," she assured him, without much conviction.

Bram thanked Tyler again and left, but not without a backward glance at the two of them, as if he wasn't any more pleased to be leaving Willow alone with Tyler than to be leaving her alone at all.

Once they had watched Bram and the deputies drive off, Tyler said, "Come on. I'll help you clean up."

Willow knew she should decline the offer. Tyler had done enough. But since the last thing she wanted was to go up to that apartment by herself, she said a simple,

"Thanks," of her own and led the way back up the stairs.

She was surprised to find herself reluctant to go in when she got to the landing, though. Suddenly she had a flash of what had happened, of stepping through the door and being grabbed from behind.

Maybe her fear showed on her face, because as she stood there staring at the door rather than going through it, Tyler took her hand and said, "It's okay now, but let's go in together, anyway." And then he opened the screen and went in first.

In the commotion, Willow hadn't realized just what a mess her apartment was. But that initial glance around shocked her.

The ice cream had opened when she'd dropped it, splattering everywhere and then melting into a puddle. Cupboard doors were open and shelves spilled their contents. Drawers were pulled completely out of their slots. Her pantry looked as if it had suffered an avalanche.

And apparently that was only the beginning, because when she looked out into the living room she could see furniture upturned, pillows and cushions everywhere, tables tossed aside, lamps on their sides on the floor, even one curtain rod pulled from the wall and left hanging at half-mast.

Again Tyler must have seen how overwhelmed she was, because he squeezed her hand and said, "It looks worse than it is. We'll get it all put back together in no time."

Then he let go of her, high-stepped over the debris in the kitchen and went into the living room to prove it by setting to work righting her sofa and replacing the cushions.

It still took Willow a moment to gather her wits, but when she finally did she started on the ice cream mess. When that was cleaned up she went on to replacing drawers and what was in them.

She moved as if through a haze, trying not to think about the stranger who had been in her apartment, who had gone through her things, who had terrified her. And before too long she and Tyler managed to do exactly what he'd promised—they'd put the place back together.

The only problem was that once that was finished Willow was left with the prospect of Tyler leaving. Of really being alone there.

And she realized that her brother had been right, it wasn't a good thing.

"I don't have any ice cream to offer, but would you like a glass of iced tea?" she said then, feebly looking for any excuse to get Tyler to stay a little longer.

"No, that's okay. I'm not thirsty. But I am worrying about leaving you tonight."

Willow laughed a small, uncertain laugh. "I'm worrying a little about that myself."

"Why don't I stay then? On the couch," he was quick to add. "I know I'd feel a lot better."

So would she. And while she knew she should decline that offer, too, she thought that under the unusual circumstances of the evening, maybe just this once she could admit to her own temporary weakness and give in to what would make her feel better, as well.

"Would you hate that a lot?" she asked with a small smile.

"Sleeping on your couch? I've slept in worse places. And to tell you the truth, I don't see myself resting if I'm *not* here tonight."

"Then I'm going to take you up on it," she confessed.

"Good."

His smile showed his relief, and Willow was sure he had no ulterior motives.

"I even think I have a pair of Logan's pajama bottoms. He spent a few nights here when his place was being painted, and left them," she said, going to the hall closet for those and for bedding to make up the sofa.

She felt relieved, too, to know Tyler would be there. It was just that the idea of it, of Tyler being right outside her bedroom door all night long, made her feel other things, too. Especially when she began to think about him taking off his clothes.

About him being in nothing *but* the pajama bottoms.

Right outside her bedroom door.

All night long.

Then something hot and sparkling kicked up in the pit of her stomach to go with the relief.

"You can change in the bathroom," she told him

as she finished with the couch, trying to keep her mind off the image of him undressing.

Tyler took the pajama bottoms into the other room, and as he did Willow put some effort into getting a grip on herself.

The best thing to do, she decided, was to get ready for bed as if this were no big deal, say a fast goodnight and get to sleep as quickly as possible.

So, while Tyler was in the bathroom, she went into her bedroom.

Oversize T-shirts were what she ordinarily slept in. Plain, sexless T-shirts. She didn't own anything else. So that was what she yanked on over her head.

Then she brushed her hair to free it of the tangles it had gathered in her tussle with Kenny Randolph, and added a short terry-cloth bathrobe she cinched at the waist—also plain and completely unsexy.

No chance of Tyler thinking she wanted to seduce him, she concluded after a glance in the mirror.

And that was good, because she *didn't* want to seduce him.

Although she was having trouble not thinking about how blissful it had been when he'd joined her outside earlier tonight and held her in his arms. Or how nice it would be to have him do it again...

"Are you decent?" she called through the closed bedroom door.

"Decent," he confirmed from the living room.

Willow went out there, bracing herself for that first sight of him.

But even preparation didn't help.

Because there he was, in only the baggy pajama bottoms, his upper half bare. And that flat stomach, that hard-muscled chest, those broad shoulders were too glorious a sight not to admire. Not to want to reach out and touch.

"Are you all set out here?" she asked in a voice left weak from that one glimpse of him.

"I think so," he answered.

She thought he was being very careful not to look below her chin.

"I'm usually up pretty early, so I can wake you anytime you want."

"Whenever you get up is fine. I don't have a time clock to punch."

"Okay. Well. I should probably say good-night."

Tyler agreed with a tilt of his chin. But he didn't merely stand there. He took her hand much as he had earlier and said, "I'll walk you to your door."

Willow laughed at that. "You'd better. Look what happens when you don't. Bad guys pop out at me from the shadows."

He ushered her to the bedroom door, facing her when they got there, looking down into her eyes.

"Thanks for a nice night," he joked, as if this were a normal ending to a normal evening.

"Sure," she joked back.

"It's the most excitement I've had since I quit rodeoing."

"That was my plan."

He grinned on only the dimpled side. "So this was all just for my entertainment?"

"It was."

"I always like a girl full of surprises."

"Oh, I hope so," she heard herself say before she realized she was going to.

But in the spirit of their teasing banter Tyler didn't seem to have any inclination how much she meant that.

He just went on looking into her eyes, drawing her into the emerald-green depths of his and warming her to her toes.

Then he leaned forward and kissed her. Chastely. With their bodies still far apart, only their lips meeting.

It was sweet that he was being so conscientious, so considerate. But Willow wanted more. She needed more.

It was as if the scare of the earlier hours had left her hovering somewhere inside herself, and Tyler alone could bring her out again, bring her to life. If only he would go back to treating her like a flesh and blood woman.

Almost on their own her hands went to his neck. His strong, thick neck. Pulling him slightly nearer and deepening the kiss herself.

Deepening it so much that Tyler got the message and wrapped his arms around her as if something inside him had finally been unleashed, too, and he couldn't refrain from enfolding her in that embrace, from pulling her closer still so that she was pressed against him the way she wanted to be.

But it was only a moment before he stopped kissing her so he could look into her face once more, into her eyes, as if to be sure he was reading her signals right.

His question showed only in the lifting of his eyebrows, but she knew what he was thinking. That she'd stopped things between them the night before because she didn't want them to move too fast. Yet here they were, almost instantly picking up where they'd left off, with passion ready to erupt all over again.

She thought about the wisdom of letting this go further as she looked back up at his amazingly handsome face, as she ran her fingertips along his cheek and dipped one into that crease that made it so distinctive.

And while she knew she'd kept that passion from finding completion the previous night because she'd thought that the real Willow wouldn't go as far as making love with Tyler, she now thought that when she was with him the real Willow was different than she'd ever been before. That she was part old Willow and part Wyla. And this new Willow she'd become wanted too badly to make love with him to deny herself.

So all she did was smile. A small smile that answered that questioning arch of his eyebrows. That let him know that tonight she wouldn't stop anything.

"You're sure?" he asked anyway.

She nodded.

And that was all the go-ahead he needed.

He kissed her again, but this time it was an eager kiss as lips relaxed and parted. One kiss turned into two, into three, awakening a hunger in Willow that seemed to have been waiting just below the surface since that night in Tulsa all those weeks ago. A hunger that had been reawakened the previous evening and was now full and intense.

She let her hands go from Tyler's neck to his back, losing herself in the feel of power kept in check. In the feel of that strong back bending to her will.

He deserted her mouth to kiss her neck, and his breath against her skin was warm and soft before he reclaimed her mouth with lips parted farther still. He sent his tongue to fence with hers, and she met his every thrust with a gleeful parry of her own.

She loved the smell of him. The clean scent of his skin and his aftershave mingling.

She loved the feel of his skin. Silk over steel.

She loved the feel of his big hands on her, too. Holding her. Rubbing her back. Kneading it the way she longed for him to knead her oh-so-engorged breasts. Caressing it in a way that soothed, that adored, that aroused.

He looped his arm under hers and took her shoulder in his hand from behind, using his biceps to raise her arm. The sleeves of her T-shirt and robe fell away. And then somehow he had her robe untied and he slipped it off, leaving it to fall at her feet on the hall floor.

He held her hand in his and took her into the bedroom, where the lamp on the nightstand lent a faint, milky glow.

Willow wished she were wearing something more enticing than her plain white T-shirt, and in the hopes of adding even just a hint of allure, she moved to turn off the light.

But Tyler stopped her, pulling her back with him onto the bed.

"I want to see you."

As with times before, it was a small thing. But knowing he couldn't care less about what she was wearing, that he found her enticing and alluring all on her own, did wonders for Willow. She clamped her arms around his neck and smiled up at him, knowing all the more that she wanted him.

He kissed her again then. As softly, as tenderly as the first time, and yet with a new depth that made everything inside her stand up and take notice.

Everything inside her and her nipples, too, as they hardened into tight kernels of yearning, crying out for his attention.

But from that moment on Tyler anticipated her every want, her every need. No sooner was she struck by the urge to have his hand on her breast than Tyler did exactly that—first on the outside of her T-shirt and then underneath it, gifting her with the glory of his naked touch.

No sooner did she crave the freedom of being without any barriers between them than he slipped her T-shirt off, looking down at her as if she were the most beautiful woman he'd ever seen as he shucked the pajama bottoms and allowed her the view of him in all his tumescent magnificence.

Magnificence that made her glad the light was on, that made her lose all inhibitions, all self-consciousness when she realized how much of an effect she was having on him. When she began to revel in the sight of chiseled muscles, taut tendons and pure masculine perfection.

Their kisses grew more than hungry. They grew urgent and openmouthed as his hands turned her breasts into mounds of pleasure so intense it was nearly too much to bear.

Then his mouth began a purposeful descent. To kiss her chin. To kiss the hollow of her throat. To flick the very tip of his tongue against the sharp ridge of her collarbone. To touch it again to the spot between her breasts before he finally reached one straining orb.

He took it into the hot moist cove of his mouth, teasing her nipple. Circling it. Flicking at it. Teasing and tormenting until he made her spine arch with delight. With yearning. With the craving for even more.

Willow's hands had been traveling, too. Exploring his carved and cut back, his Herculean shoulders, his exceptional chest, even his taut derriere. But now, as desire coursed through her, a new brazenness took hold and she reached for that long, hard staff that proved how much he wanted her.

This time it was Tyler whose spine arched, who

gave a ragged moan that let her know she wasn't the only one lost in the sensations of the flesh, in the pleasure.

Pleasure he offered her more of when his hand trailed south, too. When he reached between her legs to find the core of her and drive her to a new frenzy until she thought she might explode if she didn't have him inside her.

And that, too, Tyler seemed to know.

He deserted her for just a moment then, returning sheathed to lie on his back and pull her on top of him, guiding her hips, slipping fully into that waiting home that seemed fashioned for him alone.

Then he eased her into a sitting position.

"Let me see you," he said again, his voice deep and raspy.

His hands on her hips once more helped her, raising her up and down. Slowly. Rhythmically. Showing her how to ride before increasing the speed, the energy, the force. Until their bodies moved in unison, melded into one, straining, striving for the same thing. For that culmination that felt to Willow like a blown-glass bubble bursting open to rain glittering gold all through her, suspending them both in that instant of exquisite bliss that snatched her breath and his, that stopped the world from turning and time from passing until all that glittering gold began to settle like tiny sparkling stars drifting to earth.

And when they were both spent, Tyler pulled her down to him, holding her, pressing her head to his chest where she could hear his heart pounding in unison with hers.

They stayed that way for a long while. Speaking only with bodies that met and meshed as if one began where the other ended.

Then Tyler reached to turn off the bedside lamp and they rolled together to their sides, arms and legs entwined, Willow's forehead against his chest, his chin atop her head.

And that was how they remained as exhaustion began to weigh them down. As they both drifted to sleep.

With their baby snuggled safely, secretly, between them.

And Willow knowing that she truly wasn't the same person she'd been before she met Tyler that night in Tulsa.

Chapter Nine

In the heat of the moment the night before, Willow
had forgotten about the morning sickness. But like
clockwork, at 5:00 a.m. it hit. And waking up in Tyler's arms didn't keep it at bay.

The best she could do was ease herself away from
him and out of the bed without waking him, and then
run like crazy for the bathroom.

Ordinarily, once the first wave passed she went back
to bed and tried to get a little more sleep. But she was
afraid she'd disturb Tyler if she did, so she picked up
her bathrobe from the hall floor, put it on and curled
up in the wing chair near the living room window to
watch the sunrise.

And to think about what she was going to do now.

Making love with Tyler again was a big step. It changed things. It somehow made not telling him about Tulsa seem less acceptable.

Besides, if her goal had been to get him to like her for who she really was, that seemed to have been accomplished. After all, he liked her well enough to ask to see her repeatedly. He liked her enough to kiss her. To do more than kiss her. He liked her enough to fight off Kenny Randolph. To help her clean the mess the other man had left. To stay the night so she'd feel safe.

He liked her enough to make love to her.

To make love to her the way he'd made love to her as Wyla.

He even seemed to like her enough to stick around after meeting her brothers.

It seemed that all of that was proof that she hadn't merely been a one-night stand for him. That she hadn't been someone he'd been attracted to because of a supershort slinky dress, a pair of spike-heeled shoes, and hair and makeup that had transformed her into something she wasn't.

And since, after getting to know each other, they'd ended up in exactly the same place they had that one night, she thought that must surely mean that one night hadn't merely been a fluke.

Besides, now that she knew Tyler better, that really did seem unlikely. After all, he was a stand-up guy. He was kind and compassionate and considerate and caring, on top of being fun to be with and interesting and brave enough not to be cowed by her brothers or an intruder.

That night they'd been together in Tulsa might have been purely a night of wild abandon, of passion. Of potent physical attraction. But now it seemed as if there was more between them.

At least there was more on Willow's side.

She didn't want to admit it, but she had feelings for Tyler. Feelings she refused to put a name to. Feelings she was trying hard to keep boxed up until she knew what was going to happen.

But even realizing she had to be cautious couldn't stop her from hoping that all the time Tyler had wanted to spend with her, the attraction he seemed to have for her, were signs that there was more on his side, too. Maybe even feelings that would match her own.

Yet whether or not that was the case, she was suddenly convinced that the time had come to tell him the truth. About Tulsa. And about the consequences of that night together.

Not that it was going to be easy, and the morning's second lurch of her stomach warned her it wasn't a chore she was eager to perform.

But it was still something she had to do.

She'd already been carrying his baby for two months without him knowing it. She'd already pushed the envelope by not filling in his memory about Tulsa. Now there was no way out of it. She had to be honest with him. Open with him. She had to tell him. To explain it all.

And then she'd just have to keep her fingers crossed that after some inevitable shock, he would accept it. That he might even be happy about it.

That maybe they could go on from there.

Although she was afraid to think about where she actually might want to go from there.

But one thing she was pretty sure about.

If she told Tyler about Tulsa and the baby, and he turned his back on her, it was going to hurt more than anything had ever hurt before.

It was 6:30 when Tyler woke up to find himself alone in Willow's bed.

He doubted that she'd left for work yet, and thought she was probably just letting him sleep while she showered or dressed or made breakfast.

But he started wondering if he might be able to lure her back to bed, and with that in mind, he got up, pulled on the pajama bottoms she'd lent him and went in search of her.

He was surprised at where he found her, though.

She wasn't showering or dressing or making breakfast. She was in a chair in the living room, her feet tucked underneath her, her head against the chair's wing back, sound asleep.

He couldn't figure out why she would have left the bed—and him—to sleep sitting up in a chair. But it worried him a little. Maybe she'd been regretting that they'd made love.

If that were the case he wasn't sure he wanted to face what might be recriminations without his pants on. So he decided to exchange the pajama bottoms for his jeans, making sure to be quiet so he didn't wake her until he was ready.

Off went the pajamas, tossed over the arm of the sofa, before he reached for his jeans, which were folded neatly on the end table. Then he sat on the couch, still made up as his makeshift bed, and began to pull on his retrieved denims.

But as he did he caught sight of Willow again, and he couldn't tear his eyes away.

She was sleeping so peacefully. With her mouth open just the slightest bit, as if she might be about to blow out birthday candles. Her long, dark eyelashes rested against her cheeks and the morning sunshine coming through the window dusted her skin in a pale glow.

But something about the way she looked, bathed in that early sunshine, caused what felt like a brain blip in him.

A brain blip that started to flash images through his mind.

Images of Willow.

But not Willow.

Images of her sleeping the way she was now, but not sitting up in a chair.

In a bed.

On the pillow next to him.

But not in *her* bed. Not on the pillows he'd just left behind.

Not here.

In a hotel room.

Willow.

But not Willow?

The same long, silky black hair framing the same face. The same high, broad cheekbones. The same satin-smooth, flawless skin. The same full, luscious lips.

Willow?

Wyla...

That was her name! Wyla! The name of the woman he'd spent that night in Tulsa with. The name of the mystery woman.

Wyla.

Willow.

It all came back to him suddenly. That night. Meeting the beautiful, raven-haired woman at the blues club.

Her friend had introduced her as Wyla. Wyla from Black Arrow. Then her friend had left them alone.

They'd hit it off. Instantly. It had been as if they'd known each other all their lives—that was how comfortable he'd felt with her.

She'd had a lot to drink.

He'd kissed her.

He'd wanted to never stop kissing her.

One thing had led to another and they'd ended up

in his hotel suite. In his bed. For a wild night of love-making like nothing he'd ever experienced before.

At dawn, as the first daylight had flooded across the bed, he'd slowly come awake to find her on the pillow next to his. Still sleeping.

For a long while he'd watched her. Then he'd roused her with teasing kisses and made love to her once more. Sweet, playful love that had worn them out all over again.

But while he'd slept that second time, she'd disappeared.

She'd slipped out of bed just the way she'd slipped out of bed this morning.

But he hadn't found her sitting up in another room. He hadn't been able to find her anywhere in the hotel. He hadn't been able to find her at all.

And he'd been so preoccupied with thoughts of her, with thoughts of where she might have gone, so preoccupied with looking into the crowded arena where the rodeo was being held in hopes of spotting her in the stands, that he hadn't been concentrating the way he should have been on his ride.

So preoccupied that he'd been thrown from that horse.

Wyla...

Willow.

His memory rushed back just the way he'd believed it would if he ever found the mystery woman.

His mystery woman...

Willow.

He'd figured if he met up with the mystery woman again and one look at her didn't bring back his memory, at least she would recognize him and tell him who she was. She would fill in that gap that he'd so badly wanted filled.

But Willow hadn't done that.

Why the hell *hadn't* she?

How could she not have?

Thoughts of luring her back to bed evaporated, and Tyler plunged his feet into his boots, feeling as if he'd been sucker-punched, and not too sure what to do about it.

He was tempted to storm out of there, to leave her in the dust, full of questions the way she'd left him that morning in Tulsa. The way she'd left him full of questions ever since, knowing everything and telling him nothing.

But tempted or not, he couldn't leave. Not before he found out what was going on. What game she was playing. And why.

He took a deep breath, knowing he needed to get some control over himself, over his temper, before he woke her and confronted her.

But, as if his anger had infused the air in the room and sounded an alarm for her, Willow opened her eyes just then.

She blinked, looking disoriented.

Then she noticed him sitting on the sofa.

Surprise and maybe a touch of embarrassment ran

across her face briefly, chased away by a soft, warm smile.

"Hi," she said, so sweetly it was difficult to believe it was only a front for whatever it was she had up her sleeve.

Tyler couldn't sit still. He lunged to his feet and faced her as he would have anyone who had set out to make a fool of him.

"Why didn't you tell me from the start? The first day? At the store?"

Willow's smile faded and her expression grew confused. But only slightly. Then she looked more panicked than anything.

"Yeah, that's right, my memory is back. *Wyla.*"

She hadn't had much color in her face before, but what little there had been drained out of it.

"Oh." That was all she seemed able to manage by way of a comment. Then she followed it up with, "When?"

"Just now. Watching you sleep in the sun. I watched you that next morning in Tulsa, too. Before you walked out without a word and left me thinking about how I was going to find you instead of paying attention to what I was doing on the back of that bucking bronco that day."

The stab of his words made her flinch almost imperceptibly.

She lowered her feet to the floor and sat up straight in the chair, not cowering from Tyler's looming stance in front of her.

"I'm sorry," she said, her apology sounding as if it was heartfelt, yet still not enough to soothe Tyler.

She must have seen that in him because she went on to explain. "I'd never in my life spent the night with someone I'd just met. I'd only ever slept with one other person, period. When I woke up later that morning and you were still sleeping, I couldn't believe what I'd done, and my first instinct was to just get out of there so I didn't have to face you. I was operating on pure reflex, Tyler. Please try to understand. I didn't mean to do anything to hurt you. I was just so ashamed of myself."

"So ashamed of yourself that when I walked into the Feed and Grain last week and you realized I didn't remember you, you figured you'd just go on leaving me in the dark so you could pretend it never happened?"

"I couldn't pretend it never happened," she said under her breath.

"So what were you doing? Just playing me?"

"I wasn't *playing* you."

"Then what the hell were you doing?" he shouted.

"I was just so shaken to see you again. And then I was shocked when I figured out that you didn't even recognize me. I mean, I knew I looked different. That night in Tulsa my friend Becky had fixed me up like I'd never been fixed up before. The hair, the makeup, the dress... And then she'd introduced me as Wyla— that was her nickname for me. But still I hadn't thought I was so different that you wouldn't even know me. And then, when it sank in that you really didn't remember me—before I found out about the amnesia—it was such a blow to think that I'd just been a one-night stand. Someone you'd picked up in a bar the way you'd probably picked up so many women that you couldn't even remember them all... Well, that was so humiliating I just couldn't make myself say anything.''

''And then when you found out about the fall and the amnesia?'' he demanded. ''What was the excuse then?''

She flinched again at the verbal jab.

In a small, quiet voice, she said, ''Then I decided that I wanted to see if I could get you to like me as Willow. As who I really am rather than as Becky's creation-for-a-night. I thought that by my not telling you, you'd have a chance to get to know me and I'd have a chance to get to know you.''

''And that was so damn important you figured it was all right to leave me grasping at straws, trying to get my memory back?''

''I didn't know that was what you were doing. I thought you had pretty much accepted the memory problem.''

Okay, so maybe he hadn't actually let her in on the fact that he'd been searching for the mystery woman in hopes of retrieving his memory, too. But at that moment he was too angry to take any of the blame onto himself.

''You should have told me we'd met before. That

we'd spent the night together. All you would have had to do after that was tell me that night had been a lark for you. That you wanted me to get to know you on your own terms. What the hell would have been wrong with that?''

"I know that seems reasonable enough. But I had so much riding on you liking me.''

"What does that mean? What did you have riding on it?''

She looked away from him as if she couldn't bring herself to meet his eyes, and he saw her cheeks color.

He also saw strain pull her features, and it made him wonder why it was so vital that he like her. What it could be that seemed to cause a new shame.

And then it struck him.

There was really only one thing he could think of.

"You got pregnant that night," he said, more to himself than to her.

She still didn't look at him. But she nodded her head. Just once.

"Oh my—"

"I couldn't just blurt it all out when you didn't even know who I was," she said quietly, still staring out the window rather than at him. "You didn't remember me. Or that night. How could I—"

"You're pregnant? You're really pregnant?" His own disbelief made his voice loud enough to echo through the house.

Willow swallowed hard. "I have the morning sickness to prove it," she said, making a feeble attempt at a joke.

Tyler jammed his fingers into his hair, ending up with his forehead in his palm as he shook his head, trying hard to absorb all this.

"You should have told me. Why the hell didn't you tell me?" he repeated, again more to himself than to her, feeling as if he were having a bad dream.

"Believe me, I wish I'd had a chapter in *Miss Manners* that told me what to do. But I didn't. If there wasn't a baby, maybe it would have been easier. Maybe then I could have just said, *Hey, remember me?* But the baby put a whole different spin on it. I couldn't just casually remind you of that night and then say, *Oh, and by the way, I ended up pregnant.* The whole subject, the whole situation was delicate, and I just thought that maybe I could ease you into it. Either into remembering me and that night in Tulsa, or at least into liking me a little, knowing me a little, before you got the whole thing sprung on you."

"So you were only thinking of me," he said facetiously.

"I told you, I didn't know how to handle it! I don't know who would."

The rise and fall in her voice revealed her frustration. But Tyler was too buried in his own mire to feel sympathy for her. In fact, this whole thing had hit him like a ton of bricks, and he didn't know what to think, what to feel, how else to react.

He stood and grabbed his shirt. "I have to get out of here."

Willow finally looked at him again, with doe eyes full of fear and confusion and disappointment and disillusionment—all things that only added to what he couldn't deal with at that moment.

He could only say, "I'm not walking out on you or turning my back on you or the baby, or anything like that. I just need some air. Some time to sort through this whole thing. Then I'll be in touch."

He'd be in touch....

That sounded bad.

But he couldn't help it. He couldn't get over the fact that she'd lied to him this entire time. That she'd strung him along.

That she was pregnant on top of everything else.

And he knew that anything more he said might make matters worse.

So he didn't say anything at all.

And neither did Willow.

In fact, she didn't even go on looking at him.

Instead, she turned her head away again.

And Tyler had the sense that she'd closed the door on him even before he'd left.

Chapter Ten

Hours later, Willow was still sitting in the chair by the window. Still wearing only her bathrobe. Still feeling sick enough to warrant having called downstairs to the Feed and Grain to tell Carl she wasn't going to work today.

But by then her illness was less morning sickness and more heartsickness.

And the last thing she needed was for her brother Bram to come up the stairs from the store and let himself and Jenna into her apartment just after noon.

"Willow? Carl says you're up here sick. Is that true?" Bram called even before he'd found her in the chair.

"Just a little under the weather," she answered, as her brother and her friend came into the living room.

Jenna didn't hesitate to cross to her, sitting on the window ledge and immediately pressing a hand to her forehead.

"No fever," she announced as she went on to take Willow's pulse.

"I'll be all right," Willow assured them. "A day of rest and I'll be good as new."

Bram frowned down at her, but seemed to have too many things on his own mind to delve any more deeply into her health problems. Instead he began going from window to door to window, making notes and talking as he went.

"Those lousy state police let Kenny Randolph get away from them," he said, agitation ringing in his tone. "Looks like he was headed west, probably back to California, but I don't like that he's on the loose again. And since I know it won't do any good to try to get you to stay with me until Randolph gets picked up, I'm sending one of my deputies over here later to put heavy-duty bolts on your windows and doors. On the windows and doors downstairs, too."

Willow was too distraught to care much about Kenny Randolph. "He knows I don't have the papers. I doubt he'll come back here," she said.

"I talked to Rand Colton this morning and told him about Randolph breaking in. He had me contact his father, Joe Colton. Joe and Graham Colton are brothers, and Rand thinks that since we're apparently dealing with someone with a connection to Graham, Joe might be able to get to the bottom of this whole thing quicker than Rand could. He may be right, because when I called Joe Colton he guaranteed me he'd start an investigation of his own, beginning with having a talk with his brother.''

''Good,'' Willow said, as Bram passed from the bedrooms through the living room and on into the kitchen.

In the silent pause after Bram announced that he needed a glass of water, Jenna whispered, ''Are you having your normal morning sickness or is something more wrong?''

''Something more is wrong, but it isn't with the baby,'' Willow whispered back. ''Tyler regained his memory.''

''And he's not happy that you didn't tell him who you were before?'' Jenna guessed.

''*Not happy* is putting it mildly.''

''Did you tell him about the baby, too?''

Willow nodded. ''He wasn't happy about that, either. He said he had to get out of here and that's what he did.''

''Prenatal vitamins? What the…'' Bram's voice interrupted their quiet talk as he stepped into the archway that connected the living room and the kitchen. He had in his hand the telltale bottle Willow had put in the cupboard above the sink. The same cupboard where she kept the water glasses, so she'd see the vitamins and remember to take them.

''Are these yours?'' her brother asked.

Willow wondered if maybe she was just being punished all the way around today.

Jenna gave her a concerned, panicked look, and suddenly Willow didn't have the energy to fight the inevitable any longer. "Yes, they're mine," she admitted.

"You're pregnant?" Bram said, even more loudly and more shocked sounding than Tyler.

"Yes."

"How? Who?"

"I think you know how, Bram," Jenna said, trying to lighten the atmosphere.

It didn't work.

"Who? When?" Bram amended.

Jenna was holding Willow's hand, lending her support as Bram came to stand in much the same place Tyler had that morning.

But all the support in the world didn't matter when, as if she were helping Willow by answering for her, Jenna said, "Tyler Chadwick is the father."

Willow cringed. "Oh, you shouldn't have told him," she nearly moaned.

"I thought you were coming clean," Jenna said apologetically.

"Tyler Chadwick?" Bram repeated venomously. "He's only been in town a couple of weeks."

Jenna looked to Willow, cautious now.

But Willow merely shrugged, letting her friend know she might as well tell the rest.

With that go-ahead, Jenna said, "They met in Tulsa.

In June.'' She went on to explain it all to Bram, while Willow wished she could crawl into a hole and never come out.

By the time Jenna had finished, Bram's balled-up fists were on his hips. ''Son of a—''

''Please,'' Willow said then, recognizing the signs that her brother was about to go into protective mode. ''Just leave it alone, Bram.''

''Leave it alone? I'm not leaving anything alone. You're *pregnant,* for crying out loud. And this guy—''

''This guy nothing,'' Willow said, somehow finding a surge of strength to put some force into her voice. ''The baby is mine. I made the decision to have it, to raise it, on my own. And that's all there is to it. What happens—or doesn't happen— between Tyler and me is *only* between Tyler and me, and I want you to stay out of it.''

Apparently a lifetime of Willow pussyfooting around her brothers hadn't prepared Bram for the bluntness in her tone, because he just stood there, staring at her with an even more shocked look on his face.

But Willow knew the moment had come for her to finally take a firm stand, and now that she'd begun she was going to stick to it.

''You're a good brother, Bram,'' she said. ''But this is my business and my business alone. I've handled it up to now and I'll go on handling whatever happens from here on. Just be happy that you're going to be an uncle and forget about everything else.''

"Forget about everything else?" he parroted, as if she were asking for the moon.

"Yes," Willow said decisively. "It's time you accept that I'm a grown woman. That I can take care of myself and that this is my life."

"If you've gone and let yourself get pregnant without being married, you haven't taken such good care of yourself up till now."

"Bram!" Jenna cried.

"Well it's true, isn't it? And what about this guy? He has responsibility here. What's he going to do about it?"

"I'll say it again—that's my business, not yours," Willow stated in a deadly calm tone. "I mean it, Bram. You're not my champion and I want you to stay completely, totally out of this. You're Switzerland. You're neutral. And I'm not kidding."

But apparently even taking a stand didn't have any effect on her brother.

Because, much as Tyler had done earlier, he merely turned on his heel and walked out of the apartment, leaving both Jenna and Willow in his wake.

For a long while Tyler just plain didn't know what to do with himself. He paced and paced some more. He showered and shaved. He got dressed for the day. Then he paced all over again.

He couldn't eat, not breakfast or lunch. He wasn't hungry. He couldn't sit still. He couldn't work or even watch television.

.

And he couldn't think about anything but Willow.

Willow being his mystery woman. Willow keeping that information from him. Willow pregnant.

In the last two months since the fall in Tulsa, he'd pictured a hundred times how meeting up with his mystery woman might play out. About how he'd feel. About where it might lead.

But never had he imagined that it would tick him off.

Of course, he hadn't imagined that it would involve his mystery woman being pregnant, either.

Not that that was what had him hot under the collar. That wasn't even something he could really fathom yet.

It was Willow's deception he was honed in on. Willow's deception that he just couldn't seem to get past.

Sick of pacing the house, Tyler kicked open the screen door and went out onto the front porch, hiking a foot up on the top of the railing and leaning his elbow on his upraised thigh.

He wished he had someone to hash this out with, to be his sounding board. But he didn't want to call his brother. He didn't want to admit to Brick that he'd been had—because that's what this felt like.

He knew Brick had thought all along that he should give up on his obsession with finding his mystery woman. That he should just move on with his life and forget about her. Now Tyler didn't want to run even the small risk that Brick would say *I told you so,* and that meant Tyler couldn't talk to him.

He was on his own. But it was driving him a little crazy.

A slight breeze set the porch swing swaying and the creak of the chains that held it made Tyler have another flash of memory, this one not of things he'd forgotten, but of only a few days ago. Of sitting on that porch swing with Willow.

He glanced over his shoulder at the swing, half expecting to see her there.

Half wanting to see her there.

And that gave him pause.

He was furious with her. How could he be wishing she was there with him?

But he was. If he looked deep inside himself, if he looked beyond the anger and outrage, he was still wishing she were there.

His thoughts about his brother's point of view popped back into his head. But with a slightly different twist.

Brick had thought Tyler should give up on his drive to find his mystery woman. But what if what he gave up on was his anger over the way it had finally happened? What if the anger was what he let go of?

Then what?

Tyler thought about that. Seriously.

Letting go of the anger was easier said than done. Letting go of his injured pride was easier said than done, too.

But staying mad, nursing his injured pride, didn't seem like a wise choice for the long run.

And what would he have left when that anger and injured pride died of natural causes?

Not Willow, that was for sure.

And he realized that not having Willow in his life was not a scenario he liked.

She shouldn't have done what she did. She shouldn't have pretended they didn't know each other. She shouldn't have left him floundering for something that she held in the palm of her hand.

But what had she said in explanation of it all?

That she'd been confused herself. That she'd felt humiliated to think he hadn't remembered her or that night they'd spent together in Tulsa.

It must have been terrible for her, he admitted then, to have come face-to-face with him and not have him know who she was. It must have been insulting and demoralizing. Made even worse by the fact that she was pregnant by a person who didn't so much as recall having ever met her before.

Now that he thought about it, it was amazing she hadn't thrown something at him.

But she hadn't. Not Willow. She hadn't struck out at him at all.

Instead she'd opted for using the unusual circumstances of his amnesia to the best advantage. She'd used them to let him get to know her.

And what had he gotten to know about her? he asked himself.

Not that she was ordinarily secretive and deceitful, that was for sure.

Until this morning he'd believed she was kind and compassionate and honest and aboveboard. In fact, he'd seen for himself that she was all those things. Along with being pleasant and even-tempered. With being beautiful and fun to be with and sexy and everything he'd always wanted in a woman.

Had he been wrong?

His injured pride wanted to think he had been. That he'd been wrong about her and wronged by her.

But again he couldn't help thinking that she might have used the unusual circumstances she'd been faced with to the best advantage. After all, because of what she'd done, they'd been allowed to get to know each other in a natural way. Without the shadow of that night they'd spent together. Without the pressure of him knowing there was going to be a baby because of it.

Now that he considered that, it occurred to him that might have been pretty smart of her. Certainly it had left him more free than he would have felt had she told him the whole thing from the get-go.

So maybe leaving him in the dark hadn't been such a bad choice. Maybe it had actually given him an unfettered opportunity he wouldn't have had otherwise. An opportunity, just as she'd said, to learn who she really was. To like her for who she really was.

To more than like her…

Yeah, he did more than like her, he admitted to himself. In fact, what he felt about her was a lot more than liking.

But could he forgive her?

Maybe a better question was how could he *not* forgive her? he thought as he finally began to calm down and think straight.

Nothing terrible had come from her not letting him know they'd had that night in Tulsa. The only terrible thing that could come of it was if he *did* hold it against her. If he let it destroy what had started between them twice now.

And it would be his fault if he let that happen.

So he wasn't going to.

He wasn't going to go against what he really wanted, deep down, beneath the impulses of his anger and injured pride.

Because what he really wanted was Willow.

And he needed to see her, to tell her, to work this whole thing out with her, he realized.

Which was just what he was going to do.

If she'd still let him after he'd deserted her this morning.

Tyler pushed off the porch railing and backtracked to close his front door.

But by the time he'd done that and turned to head for his truck, two other trucks and the sheriff's car were coming up the drive from the main road.

And before he knew it, he was facing all four of Willow's brothers.

* * *

The possibility of one of Bram's deputies showing up to put bolts on her doors and windows finally got Willow out of the chair by the window about an hour after she'd dispatched Jenna to find Bram and keep him from whatever it was he'd bounded out of the apartment to do.

Willow still felt as if she'd been run over by a truck, but she managed to take a quick shower and shampoo her hair.

Neither the warmth of the shower spray or of the hair dryer she'd used afterward made her feel any better, and as she wrapped a towel around herself and tucked in one corner to hold it on until she picked out something to wear, she wondered if she would ever feel good again.

Then she opened the bathroom door and stepped into her bedroom, stopping in her tracks the moment she caught sight of Tyler. Sitting on the edge of the bed they'd mussed up together.

"Tyler," she said, sounding as stunned as she felt and not welcoming at all.

She raised a hand to the top of her towel, as if just the fact that he was there might cause it to spontaneously fall off.

"Hear me out before you tell me to hit the road, will you?" he said.

As a matter of fact she was half tempted to tell him

just that. In the hours since he'd left she'd been so miserable she'd thought a lot about the advantages of being on her own. Of really having and raising her baby by herself. Of not having to deal with any men at all. And she wasn't too sure that wasn't preferable. At least then she couldn't be disappointed and hurt the way she'd been this morning.

"How did you get in here?" she demanded, still considering asking him to go.

"I came up the stairs from the store."

"Alone?"

"If you mean did your brothers make me come here with a gun to my back, they didn't. They showed up at my place, but they were too late. I'd already made up my mind what I wanted."

Willow angled her chin upward. "And what is it that you want?" she asked with a challenge in her tone.

"You," he said without hesitation.

"Was that why you had to get out of here in such a hurry earlier?" she asked none too nicely.

"I know that wasn't the best thing I could have done. But you have to admit I'd had a couple of pretty big blows to deal with."

"And you dealt with them by walking out."

"Only for a little while. Can't we look at it as a cooling off period that didn't take too long? Just a breather?"

"Did you cool off?"

"I did."

He got up from the bed and came to stand in front of her. He didn't touch her, but she could feel the heat of his big body, and that went a lot further in soothing her than the shower or the hair dryer had.

Although she still wasn't sure she was happy that was the case.

"I not only cooled off," Tyler added, "but I realized a few things, too."

"Like what?"

"Like even though I still wish you would have told me the minute I walked into the Feed and Grain that we'd had that night in Tulsa together, you used my lack of memory to both our advantages. And even though I was really mad that you didn't tell me, I wasn't as mad at you as I would be at myself if I lost you over this. Plus I'm in love with you and I want you, and I wouldn't want to live the rest of my life without you."

It would have been so easy to believe all of that. But Willow couldn't help thinking about Bram having stormed out of there himself. Apparently he'd rounded up the rest of her brothers to confront Tyler, no doubt to force him to do the right thing by their unwed, pregnant sister. Which meant it was possible her brothers had orchestrated Tyler's presence here and dictated what he was to say to her to convince her he'd come on his own.

"How much did my brothers influence your realizations?"

"I told you, they were too late. I'd made up my mind before they ever got there."

"Sure you did. And there's probably not a mark on you."

Tyler yanked open the snaps that held his shirtfront closed and shed it just as quickly. "Take a look for yourself. No bruises."

He'd bared his magnificent chest, and one look at it stirred memories of the previous night, of running her hands all over his steely pectorals and iron-hard stomach. Of using his broad shoulder as the perfect pillow.

And she felt her will weaken.

Then he reached for the button on the waistband of his jeans, and Willow knew she wouldn't be able to resist him if he stripped down completely, the way he seemed intent on doing. So she stopped him.

"Okay, so no brute force was used. That just means you were smart enough to agree to what they wanted before fists flew."

"What that means is that I let them know I was on my way to propose to you, and if that's what they'd come to talk to me about they'd wasted their time."

Willow tore her eyes from his chest, fighting cravings for him and working hard to hold on to reason.

Then she shook her head. "I don't believe you."

Tyler's eyebrows arched in disbelief. "What don't you believe?"

"That you're here because you want to be. That my brothers didn't have a hand in it. That you're over your shock and anger already and want to live happily ever after as if this were some dumb fairy tale."

"Why not? You set out to let me get to know you. To see if I would like you the way you really are. Didn't I show you every step of the way that that's exactly what happened? Why else would I have kept coming back for more? Even in the face of your brothers' opposition I still stuck around, still wanted to see you."

"You didn't want to see me this morning," she reminded him.

"Even people who love each other get ticked off, Willow. But it passes and the love is still there to stay. That's what I figured out today—that even though I was mad, I still loved you. I still wanted you. Underneath it all, I still wanted you," he repeated, enunciating each word slowly as if to help it sink in. "And it doesn't have anything to do with your brothers or anything they did or said this afternoon."

"Or maybe you just think the same way they do and you're saying all of this because of the baby."

He closed his eyes and gave a little chuckle. "The baby," he breathed, as if he'd forgotten about it. "That doesn't even seem real to me yet. I'd be here, doing this same thing, saying these same things, even if there wasn't a baby.''

Again Willow shook her head. It all seemed too good to be true, and she was afraid of buying into it.

Tyler took her by the shoulders and gave her a gentle shake. "Listen to me. I couldn't remember that night in Tulsa, and still it made such an impact on me that I moved lock, stock and barrel to Black Arrow just on the off chance that I might meet up with you again. And even though I didn't recognize you when I did move here, even though I was still looking for my mystery woman, I couldn't resist you. That was all before I knew about the baby. Before I knew about anything. And *in spite* of everything. I fell in love with you in Tulsa. I fell in love with Wyla. And then, in Black Arrow, I fell in love with Willow. Wyla, Willow, they're both *you!* And I fell in love with every part of you. Every part of who you are. Crazy, madly in love with you. And if you'll let me, I'll spend the rest of my life proving it to you. One baby or two or three or a dozen, one brother or two or three or four brothers notwithstanding, I'm in love with you.''

Willow searched his eyes, thinking about all he'd said. Thinking about that night they'd spent together in Tulsa and about this time they'd had together since Tyler had been in Black Arrow. Thinking about all she'd learned about the kind of man he was.

And the combination of what ran through her mind and what she saw in those deep emerald eyes gave her a sudden insight and knowledge that he wasn't just saying any of that. He wasn't doing what he was doing because her brothers had pressured or intimidated him into it. He wasn't a man who said what he didn't mean. He wasn't a man who *could* be pressured or intimidated. He wasn't a man who did what he didn't want to do.

Yes, he was a man who would do the right thing, but that didn't necessarily mean marriage, and it certainly didn't require a declaration of love. He could just have come back here and offered to help her out financially, told her he wanted to be a part of the baby's life. That would have been the right thing, too.

So she had a realization of her own—that if Tyler was here telling her he loved her, then he must love her.

And it was a good thing, because she felt the same way he did. She loved him. And she couldn't let anything stand in the way of their being together.

"I love you, Willow," Tyler said then, as if he knew she needed to it hear it again.

This time she didn't shake her head. "Be careful, because I just might hold you to it," she said, testing.

"Good. Hold me to it. And say you'll marry me. That you'll let me have what I came here to find—my mystery woman."

"I don't know how mysterious I am."

"You've already been two different people since

I've known you. That's pretty mysterious. So say you'll marry me.''

''You're sure my brothers didn't threaten you with your life to make an honest woman of me?''

''Do you want to track them down and ask them?''

She didn't. ''Just tell me the truth.''

''The truth is that they did not threaten me and they didn't get the chance to tell me to make an honest woman of you because I cut them off at the pass by letting them know what I was up to. Now say you'll marry me.''

Willow pretended to think about it even though she'd already made up her mind. ''Okay, yes, I'll marry you,'' she finally said.

His smile was a full grin just before he kissed her, claiming her with his mouth as he wrapped his arms around her to pull her to him.

It was a deep kiss that went on and on, leaving Willow breathless and watery kneed and forgetful of all that had ever gone wrong between them as her nipples hardened against her towel, against the iron wall of his naked chest.

Then Tyler eased the kiss into shorter, teasing, playful nips instead. And between those playful kisses he said, ''You know, I got out of bed this morning and went looking for you, to bring you back to it. If the morning sickness is over and you're up to it...'' He glanced at the still unmade bed.

''The morning sickness is definitely over.'' And so

was the heartsickness, leaving Willow feeling better than she ever had in her life. "But we could have one of Bram's deputies here to play handyman any minute."

"Oh, I don't think so."

"No? Why not?"

"Because I warned your brothers not to disturb us."

"*You* warned *them?*"

"Why do you sound so surprised?"

"Because ordinarily it's my brothers who do the warning."

"Well, this time it was me."

"Hmm. And were you so sure of yourself or of me that you knew ahead of time that we'd need privacy?"

"Neither. I just said I wasn't letting you up for air until you agreed to be my wife. No matter what it took or how long."

"And they accepted that?"

Tyler's smile was one-sided and cocky. "I don't think we'll be having any more problems with your brothers. By the time we all left my place we ended up understanding each other pretty well and agreeing that I won't stick my nose into their affairs if they don't stick their noses into ours."

"And you came out of that alive?" she said with a laugh.

"You tell me," he urged provocatively, pulsing his hips against her to let her know just how alive he was.

Then he swept her up in his arms and swung her

onto the bed, leaving her towel behind and joining her on the mattress.

They made love right there and then, in broad daylight and without any inhibitions. And as Tyler explored every inch of her with wondrous hands and his magical mouth, as he aroused and cherished her—pausing with care at her middle, where their child was just beginning to grow—Willow felt a new abandon. A new freedom.

Because she knew that for the first time Tyler was making love to her as a complete woman. A person he knew and wanted.

And she loved him all the more for that.

A love that rocketed her into sensual space and set her soaring as their bodies united and formed one, sending them both into a climax so spectacular there could be no doubts left that they were meant to be together.

And when they'd settled back to earth, back to reality, and Tyler had rolled them to their sides so his weight atop her wasn't too much for her or their baby, he said again, "I love you, Willow. With all my heart."

"I love you with all my heart, too."

"Are there any more secrets you're keeping from me?"

She smiled. "No big ones. But what kind of a mystery woman would I be if I didn't have a few small ones?"

"You're going to keep me guessing just a little my whole life, aren't you?"

"Just a little."

But apparently it was all right, because Tyler gave a contented smile and closed his eyes just before he kissed her again, softly and full of a love Willow basked in.

And as she did she couldn't help thinking once more of her great-grandfather's words—that willows were meant to blossom and bloom during the brightest of midnights.

Or the brightest of afternoons.

Because as she lay in Tyler's arms, that was exactly how she felt—bright and happy and in full bloom.

* * * * *

Look out for Jesse's story continuing
THE COLTONS
series, included in a 2-in-1
volume from Silhouette Desire—
The Raven's Assignment
by Kasey Michaels.
On sale now.

SILHOUETTE®
SPECIAL EDITION™

AVAILABLE FROM 17TH OCTOBER 2003

GOOD HUSBAND MATERIAL Susan Mallery
Hometown Heartbreakers

When Kari Asbury revisited her home town she never expected to bump into ex-fiancé Sheriff Gage Reynolds. But could Kari find the courage to overcome their past and stand by the man she'd always loved?

TALL, DARK AND IRRESISTIBLE Joan Elliott Pickart
The Baby Bet: MacAllister's Gifts

Ryan Sharpe was blatantly masculine, sexy and…irresistible. He could be with anyone, but his passionate pursuit told Carolyn he wanted *only* her. Dare Carolyn believe he'd still want her when he learned her secret?

MY SECRET WIFE Cathy Gillen Thacker
The Deveraux Legacy

A secret sex-only marriage was the only way Dr Gabe Deveraux knew to help best friend Maggie Calloway have a baby. But soon Gabe was forced to admit the truth—he'd secretly loved Maggie for years.

AN AMERICAN PRINCESS Tracy Sinclair

When Shannon Blanchard won TV's hottest game show, she never dreamed that her prize of two weeks at a royal castle would change her life. Until she set eyes on tall, dark and dangerously attractive Prince Michel de Mornay…

LT KENT: LONE WOLF Judith Lyons

Journalist Angie Rose wanted to unveil the hero…the mysterious millionaire that was Lt Jason Kent. But how could she expose Jason's secrets when their passion—*her heart*—revealed they were meant to be together?

THE STRANGER SHE MARRIED Crystal Green
Kane's Crossing

Two years ago Rachel Shane's husband vanished. Then, without warning, a rugged stranger with familiar eyes sauntered into her life professing amnesia. He was *all*-male and every inch a dangerous temptation…